DOCTOR WHO
AND THE
RIBOS OPERATION

DOCTOR WHO AND THE RIBOS OPERATION

Based on the BBC television serial *The Ribos Operation* by Robert Holmes by arrangement with the British Broadcasting Corporation

IAN MARTER

No. 52
in the
Doctor Who Library

TARGET

A TARGET BOOK

published by
the Paperback Division of
W. H. ALLEN & Co. PLC

A Target Book
Published in 1979
by the Paperback Division of W. H. Allen & Co. PLC
44 Hill Street, London W1X 8LB

Reprinted 1980, 1982, 1983, 1984

Copyright © 1979 by Ian Marter and Robert Holmes
'Doctor Who' series copyright © 1979 by the
British Broadcasting Corporation

Printed in Great Britain by
Hunt Barnard Printing Ltd, Aylesbury, Bucks.

ISBN 0 426 20092 6

Chapter 1

Unwelcome Strangers

The tall loose-limbed figure, clad in voluminous shirt-sleeves and baggy tweed trousers tucked into creaking leather boots, strode around the faintly humming chamber. His nose was buried in an enormous tattered chart which he held up in front of his face with long, outstretched arms. From time to time he stopped in mid-stride and muttered unintelligibly to himself before setting off again, deep in thought, in the opposite direction.

Suddenly the chart flew out of his hands. He uttered a short bellow of pain and hopped about clutching an injured knee, his movements grotesquely reflected in the polished metal walls surrounding him. Then he stood still and glared at the hexagonal control console which pulsed and flashed in the centre of the chamber.

'Can't you look where you're going?' he cried, with a resentful frown. He picked up the chart and spread it out over the mass of switches, buttons, dials and lights which covered the buzzing console. Smoothing the crackling, curling edges with large, careful hands he pored over the maze of faded patterns printed on the thick, brittle paper. As he bent forward with a frown of intense concentration, his rugged features were dramatically illuminated in the fluorescent glow spilling over them.

Suddenly his eyes opened wide and he fixed a spot on the chart with a piercing stare.

'That's the place ...' he cried, straightening up and ruffling his shock of curly brown hair with both hands. 'The very place. We'll go and take a look at ...' His excited booming voice was cut short by a tremendous cracking sound. He whirled round, body tensed and arms at the ready, in a stylish karate stance. But the chamber was empty: he was quite alone. For a few seconds he stood there, blinking in confusion. Then he suddenly crouched on the defensive again as one of the doors leading from the chamber seemed to open slightly. All at once he broke into a broad toothy grin as he realised his mistake. Turning to the console he saw that the chart had rolled itself up with a snap into a tightly coiled tube.

'As I was saying,' he went on, seizing a broad-brimmed, rather shapeless brown felt hat from its perch on top of the tall glass cylinder which formed the centre of the control console, 'we'll go and take a look at . . .'

Once again the cheerful resonant voice stopped in mid-sentence. The tall figure looked round the chamber. 'K9?' he called, staring at the door which was ajar. Then he shrugged, and after frantically fumbling in his cluttered pockets, took out a tiny silver dog whistle and blew several blasts. His cheeks bulged and his eyes popped with the effort. The whistle made no sound, but immediately there came a distant whirring and clattering, and seconds later the door was pushed wide open. Into the chamber trundled a curious dog-like creature with metal body and head, fiercely glowing eyes and eagerly revolving antennae in place of ears.

The mechanical hound stopped with a jerk, cocked his head sharply to one side and announced in a rasping voice, 'A less extreme ultrasonic signal is quite adequate to effect summons, master.'

The tall figure glanced at the tiny whistle in his hand. 'I'm very glad to hear it, K9,' he panted, dabbing at his flushed face with a large, red and white spotted handkerchief. 'Next time I'll be sure to . . .'

'Your statement not understood, master,' retorted the robot, his circuits chattering busily. 'The signal is not audible to the human ear.'

6

The tall figure wagged a warning finger. 'I am *not* *human*,' he said firmly, 'kindly remember that.'

'You are the Doctor,' K9 replied, 'and according to my data bank that name is of human origin.'

The tall figure crouched down and tapped the robot on the muzzle. 'I didn't call you in to be argumentative, K9,' he murmured scoldingly. K9's eyes dimmed and his antennae drooped. Slowly he lowered his head. His circuits went quiet.

The Doctor sprang to his feet, cramming the battered hat on the back of his riot of curly hair. 'Listen, I've got a surprise for you,' he cried with a delighted smile. 'We are going to take a little holiday ... just the two of us.'

There was a pause while K9's circuits buzzed into activity again. 'Holiday?' he rasped, raising his head.

'Why not?' the Doctor said, striding over to the console and eagerly unrolling the chart. 'I thought we might pop over to Occhinos and bask in one of its suns for a few ...'

At that moment all the lights in the central console blacked out and the systems went dead with a dying whine. The Doctor uttered a cry of dismay and stumbled round the console in the eerie glow from K9's eyes, frantically flicking switches and pressing buttons. Nothing happened.

'There would appear to be a general systems malfunction, master,' K9 announced, trundling towards the console with antennae busily waving, his probe emerging from his muzzle, eager to help.

'Stay!' the Doctor ordered. 'Don't touch *anything*.'

Obediently K9 ground to a halt. Silently he watched as the Doctor tried in vain to locate the fault, struggling with the dead controls in the silent shadows.

'Come on, old girl,' he muttered coaxingly, 'this is no time to have one of your moods. Whatever's the matter?' After a while the Doctor gave up. He leaned over the console biting his lip and shaking his head. 'There is no interior fault as far as I can see,' he murmured, frowning across the chamber at the row of frosted-glass panes along the top of one of the doors. 'The TARDIS must be in the grip of some colossal external force.'

As he spoke, an intense amber light began to flood through into the chamber. The Doctor stared up at it, shielding his eyes as the glare grew rapidly brighter until he could no longer look. K9 was unaffected. The only sound was the steady whirr of his circuits as he quickly analysed the strange brilliance.

'Spectrum unidentifiable, master,' he suddenly rapped out.

The Doctor slowly walked towards the door. As he approached, the amber light gradually dimmed and when he reached it he was able to uncover his eyes. For a moment he hesitated. Then, with a decisive gesture, he took down a brown, three-quarter length overcoat with broad lapels and a high collar from the ornate wooden hallstand beside him, and thoughtfully put it on.

K9 gave a little whine of caution from the shadows as the Doctor adjusted his hat and braced himself to open the door.

'Stay' murmured the imposing figure, cautiously turning the brass door handle. A high-pitched shriek split the air as the door opened on its dry hinges. The Doctor clung to the handle to regain his balance as a momentary gust of warm air swept past him. Then, with his eyes narrowed to slits beneath the wide brim of his hat, he stepped carefully out of the TARDIS and into the sulphurous glow surrounding it.

The sound of running water and the chirruping of birds filled the air as the Doctor took a few hesitant paces and stopped to peer about him. He was standing in what looked like an exotic garden, filled with gigantic orchids nodding in the warm breeze, and shaded by enormous cool trees rustling overhead. Nearby, fountains sent up a cluster of bright rainbow sprays into the glistening leaves.

A faint creak of wickerwork came from beneath the weeping willow in front of him, and a gentle but sonorous voice murmured, 'Welcome, Doctor. Welcome.'

The Doctor approached and found himself staring with blinking, bewildered eyes at an elegant old gentleman dressed in an immaculate white suit, white panama hat, silk cravat and tan patent-leather boots. He was seated in a high-backed, elaborate veranda chair beside a round bamboo table, on which stood a dazzling crystal decanter filled with a rich amber liquid, and an empty crystal tumbler. In one raised hand the distinguished figure held a similar tumbler filled with the liquid, and from time to time he took a sip as he studied the Doctor with piercing blue eyes.

'We deeply regret the necessity of altering your plans, Doctor,' he said at last, 'but your presence is urgently required.'

The Doctor glanced at the idyllic scene around him and shrugged. 'Oh, that's all right,' he grinned. 'I'd gladly swap a trip to Occhinos for this little spot any day.'

The old gentleman smiled faintly, surveying the Doctor's well-worn attire and glancing briefly across at the chipped blue paintwork and cracked windows of the lop-sided Police Box from which he had just emerged. 'I am afraid that this is no holiday resort, Doctor,' he said coldly. 'You are here because you have been chosen to carry out an urgent and vital assignment.'

The Doctor looked aghast. 'You mean ... work?' he muttered.

The mysterious figure nodded gravely and took a long slow drink from the flashing tumbler. For a moment the Doctor was speechless. Then he thrust his hands deep into his overcoat pockets and stepped forward. 'Who are you anyway?' he demanded.

The old gentleman held up the tumbler in both hands and revolved it slowly back and forth, so that the Doctor was dazzled by the sharp beams of multicoloured light thrown out from its angled surfaces. 'Do you really need to ask, Doctor?'

The Doctor's jaw dropped. He snatched off his hat and bowed with dignified respect. 'If I had known ...' he began, quickly trying to tidy his unruly hair, 'if I had realised that ... that one of the Guardians ...' His voice trailed away and he stood there tongue-tied, screwing up his hat with embarrassment.

'Your assignment concerns the Key to Time,' said the Guardian sternly. 'You know of the Key to Time, Doctor?'

The Doctor nodded, his huge eyes alive with curiosity. 'The Perfect Cube which maintains the equilibrium of Time itself,' he murmured.

The Guardian leaned forward. 'It is divided into six different Segments which are scattered throughout the Universe disguised in various forms,' he said quietly. 'When the Segments are re-assembled into the Cube they embody an elemental force which is too dangerous for single being to possess.'

'Yes indeed,' agreed the Doctor. 'Much better that they should remain undisturbed and unrecognised.'

The Guardian sipped at his drink and shook his head. 'Doctor, at this very moment the forces of Chaos are disturbing the balance of the Cosmos ...'

'You don't have to tell *me*,' the Doctor cried. 'That's precisely the reason why I was going off to get away from it all.' He spread his arms in apology for his interruption as the Guardian leaned across and poured some of the liquid from the decanter into the empty tumbler.

'We require the completed Cube, Doctor,' the Guardian snapped, offering him the glass, 'with the minimum of delay. Without it we cannot prevent the Universe from being plunged into total and eternal chaos.'

'And you want me to volunteer,' the Doctor said, approaching the table and watching the Guardian like a hawk, a trace of suspicion crossing his face. The old gentleman stared back at him without speaking. 'And if I refuse?' the Doctor asked, picking up the tumbler and examining the contents warily.

'You will not refuse, Doctor.'

The Guardian's curt reply rang out with unexpected hollowness and the Doctor jumped. Quickly recovering himself, he drained the golden liquid in one gulp. 'Where do I start?' he cried.

'All that you require will be found in your ... your conveyance,' the Guardian replied with a gesture of disdain towards the TARDIS. 'You begin immediately.'

With a shrug of resignation the Doctor replaced his empty glass on the bamboo table. 'Persuasive little wine,' he murmured. 'Not a bad year at all. Thank you.' With that he turned and shuffled reluctantly towards the open door of the dilapidated Police Box.

'Oh Doctor, just before you go ...' the Guardian called in a warning tone, 'I am the White Guardian. For the sake of cosmic stability there is also a Black Guardian ...'

'Yes, I thought there might be,' the Doctor muttered gloomily, stopping and turning round in the doorway.

'The Black Guardian also seeks to possess the Key to Time—for evil purposes,' the White Guardian went on. 'You must prevent that, Doctor, whatever happens ...'

The Doctor made a low, respectful bow of farewell. When he looked up the luxuriant garden had disappeared. Only a swirling amber mist remained, and within seconds it had been swallowed up into the black void, leaving the Doctor teetering on the edge of the abyss.

By furiously rotating both arms simultaneously in reverse, the Doctor managed to keep his balance and propel himself backwards into the TARDIS microseconds before the outer door was sucked shut by the vacuum outside. Mopping his brow with the spotted handkerchief, he strode across to the control console which was buzzing and flickering into life again.

'Feeling better, old girl?' he murmured, anxiously checking the TARDIS's rapidly reviving systems. 'You must have had quite a shock ...' Just then he noticed that K9's eyes were glowing fiercely and his antennae whirring agitatedly from side to side. 'Whatever's the matter with you, K9?' he cried.

'Master: an alien presence has been detected, proximity ...' K9 began to rasp.

'Oh, it's quite all right,' the Doctor interrupted, 'harmless old character. I had a drink with him. He gave us a job.'

'Correction, master,' K9 retorted. 'The alien is ...'

'Quiet, or I'll close you down,' the Doctor ordered, engrossed in his work at the console. 'How can I be expected to tackle this unexpected assignment unless I am left in peace?'

At that moment one of the inner doors opened soundlessly.

'I am here to assist you, Doctor,' said a soft, musical voice which seemed to come from nowhere. The hem of a long white robe made of a silken material floated into the Doctor's field of vision. He looked up sharply and found himself face to face with a tall, aristocratic woman dressed entirely in white. Her dark hair was parted in the centre and swept back, falling in long curls on each side of her finely chiselled, almost Grecian face. Her eyebrows arched as she fixed the Doctor with pale, unblinking eyes fringed with delicately curved lashes. 'I am Romanadvoratrelundar,' she announced after a considerable pause.

'Well, my dear, I'm sorry but I really cannot be held responsible for *everything*,' the Doctor replied, shaking his head sympathetically and turning back to the control console.

Suddenly he straightened up again and thrust his face into that of the strange newcomer. 'Who are you?' he demanded.

K9 gave a brief whirr: 'Female humanoid, almost

certainly harmless,' he announced.

'I am Romanadvora ...' the stranger began patiently.

'Yes, I know all about your misfortunes,' the Doctor interrupted irritably, 'but who *are* you?'

The woman walked slowly and majestically round the console, her long robe flowing gracefully behind her. The Doctor watched her suspiciously. 'The Council warned me about your eccentricity,' she smiled, 'so naturally I studied your Bio-Data Record before I considered accepting the assignment ...'

'Oh, you were actually given a choice in the matter,' the Doctor muttered resentfully under his breath.

'... as your assistant.'

The Doctor's face darkened dangerously. He hunched his broad shoulders almost up to his ears and glowered. 'My *what*?' he rapped, clenching his teeth and gripping the edge of the console in a frenzy.

Completely undaunted, Romanadvoratrelundar took from beneath her robe a curious wand-like object. 'I was instructed to give you this,' she smiled. 'It will be invaluable in our task.'

The Doctor took the device and stared blankly at it for several seconds. 'Ah, yes, of course,' he murmured, 'absolutely indispensable, I quite agree.'

'It is the Locatormutor Core,' the stranger explained, 'and you are holding it upside down.'

Recovering himself, the Doctor shook his head firmly. 'When you have had as much experience of Time and Space as I have my dear, you will learn that up and down are concepts of very little importance,' he said with a condescending smile. Even so, he turned the instrument the other way up and studied it with a puzzled frown.

'When inserted into your navigation panel the Locatormutor will indicate the Space-Time Co-ordinates for the position of each Segment of the Key to Time,' the stranger explained in a patronising tone, pointing to a narrow, rough-edged socket cut into the panelling of the console.

The Doctor stared incredulously at the scorched and ragged hole among the intricate circuitry. 'Who did that?' he cried angrily, patting and stroking the damaged panel with soothing hands.

'It was arranged while you were with the Guardian,' Romanadvoratrelundar replied, with a smile of satisfaction. 'My instructions are to be of assistance at all times.'

Furiously the Doctor turned on K9: 'A fine watchdog *you* are,' he cried.

The robot's antennae waved briefly. 'I repeat: the female does not appear to be a hazard,' he said. 'My radiaprobe assisted in the operation.'

'So you're both in this together, are you?' the Doctor muttered, turning back to the console. 'Never mind, old girl; we'll soon get you patched up,' he murmured, rubbing at the blackened metal with his sleeve.

'Doctor, I may be inexperienced but I graduated from the Academy with Triple Alpha,' the tall stranger protested.

'Well, you've got a lot to learn about metallo-morpho technology, haven't you?' the Doctor muttered, as he tried to fit the Locatormutor Core into the uneven edges of the socket without success.

'I believe you achieved a Double Gamma ... on your third attempt,' Romanadvoratrelundar retorted, reaching over and turning the Doctor's hand round so that the device clicked smoothly into place. Immediately it began to bleep in erratic bursts, glowing faintly with each pulse. White-faced with anger and frustration, the Doctor turned and stared suspiciously at his new assistant.

Then he suddenly darted round the console, adjusting various instruments feverishly until the bleeps settled into a steady, regular rhythm. 'Seven seven ... eight three ... eight six ... nine,' he murmured as a series of numbers flashed up on the liquid crystal display in front of him.

'I will look up those co-ordinates, Doctor,' said the

14

new assistant, eagerly unrolling the Galactic Chart which still lay on the console.

'Cyrrhenis Minimis,' the Doctor said, without looking up.

Romanadvoratrelundar let the Chart roll itself up with a sharp snap. She stared at the Doctor in amazement. 'That is scarcely believable,' she exclaimed. 'How did you identify those co-ordinates without even consulting the Chart?'

The Doctor shrugged modestly. 'Just experience,' he grinned. 'Nothing difficult about it. You'll soon learn.' He began to stride round the console, waving his arms and holding forth in great style. He was enjoying his assistant's astonishment immensely.

'Of course, gadgetry is all very well,' he went on, 'but there is no substitute for sheer mental efficiency, my dear.' Stopping beside her, the Doctor glanced quickly round as if making sure they were not being overheard and whispered, 'What *is* going to be difficult is the conversion of the Segment back into its proper form once we find it. I don't suppose you've even considered *that*.'

'Not at all difficult, Doctor,' Romanadvoratrelundar smiled. 'The Locatormutor Core will perform that function perfectly adequately.'

The Doctor's superior smile faded instantly. He backed away round the control console and busied himself setting the Helmic Orientator on a course to Cyrrhenis Minimis. 'You'll find that it's quite impossible to do anything without the correct equipment,' he said pompously.

There was an awkward silence while the Doctor fiddled with the navigation circuits, watching out of the corner of his eye as the unwelcome female intruder wandered about the chamber, inspecting everything with a coolly critical gaze.

'Is there anything I can do, Doctor?' she suddenly asked.

'I don't suppose you can make tea?' the Doctor

15

muttered, giving the Vortex Primer an impatient thump with his fist. 'No, of course not ... they never teach you anything useful at the Academy.'

All at once the Doctor clutched at his head with both hands. 'See what I mean?' he cried. 'Gadgets and gimmickry ... one can never trust them.' And he started pacing round and round the chamber so furiously that even K9 retreated to a safer distance.

'What is it?' Romanadvoratrelundar asked anxiously, hurrying over to the console.

The Doctor flung out an arm and pointed to the Locatormutor Core bleeping monotonously away in its socket. 'That magic wand of yours has suddenly changed its mind,' he cried. 'Nine nine ... seven five ... zero seven ... four. The co-ordinates are not the same.'

The new assistant glanced at the liquid crystal Display showing the changed bearing. 'There is a perfectly logical explanation, Doctor,' she said calmly.

'Of course there is,' the Doctor snapped, switching off the Vortex Primer and aborting the take-off. The TARDIS gave a brief shudder as the Primer groaned to a stop.

'It means that no matter what or where it may be— one thing is certain,' the Doctor murmured, fixing his assistant with a penetrating stare, 'that Segment is on the *move*!'

16

Chapter 2

The Beast in the Citadel

In the city of Shurr, the main settlement located in the icy equatorial wastes of the planet Ribos in the constellation of Skythra, a fiercely gusting wind hurled flurries of snow across the rough-hewn parapet of the Citadel Tower. In the dying greenish light of the planet's distant cloud-obscured sun, two shadowy figures suddenly appeared crouching low on the flat rooftop. They were both huddled in thick shaggy furs which almost covered their faces. One was bulky and slow, but the other darted nimbly among the shadows. The larger figure emerged cautiously from the shelter of the parapet and knelt down to release the sturdy iron clasps holding the four corners of a heavy trapdoor sunk into the centre of the flat roof. He was joined by the smaller figure who was dragging a heavy object tied up in a skin sack. Together they strained to slide the thick iron plate aside, and eventually it gave with a harsh grating sound which echoed in the black shaft below.

'Careful, Unstoffe,' hissed the bulky figure, 'if we're caught here ...' At that moment a shattering chiming sound rocked the tower and boomed through the gathering darkness over the rugged white rooftops of the city—an extensive settlement of low, rough buildings bordered by undulating wind-swept tundra.

'Garron ... the Curfew!' exclaimed the small figure, frantically fumbling in the sack beside him.

Garron peered down into the shaft which shuddered with each beat of the gong. Then he turned his round fleshy face with its small crafty eyes towards the sharp, ferret-like features of his trembling companion: 'The moment it stops sounding, Unstoffe, drop the meat . . .' he murmured.

Below the Citadel Tower there was a vaulted chamber approached by means of a network of low-arched passageways running through the Citadel. In the centre of this chamber stood a massive wooden-framed cabinet with glass sides which contained the Sacred Relics of Ribos: an enormous jewelled crown, sceptres studded with precious stones, dazzling rings and ornaments, and ceremonial robes embroidered with rare metals. Lit by a single globe above, the sacred treasures cast piercing shafts of multicoloured light into the surrounding gloom.

In front of the cabinet the Captain of the Shrieve Guard stood with bowed head in obeisance to the holy objects, while half a dozen of his men completed the nightly ritual of extinguishing the other oil-globes hanging between the thick stone pillars supporting the roof. Then, as the chamber darkened and the booming vibration of the Curfew Gong rattled the glass panels in the cabinet, the Shrieves formed up on each side of their Captain and paid their respects. When the last strokes of the gong had died away, the Shrieves filed out of the Relic Chamber in silence. The Captain followed, walking backwards so that he always faced the sacred display, and then personally secured the massive wooden doors, sealing the chamber for the night. As soon as the locks had clattered home, two burly Shrieves began to turn the heavy iron winch-handle they had inserted into a socket in the chamber wall.

Inside the chamber a rectangular section of wall began to slide very slowly upwards. As the gap between its lower edge and the flagstone floor gradually increased, a stentorian breathing burst out of the darkness beyond the stone shutter. As the slab rose higher and higher the monstrous panting grew louder and nearer. Outside, the sweating Shrieves withdrew the handle after several dozen turns, and the Captain led his squad of Guards away, having posted a sentry beside the doors.

With a screeching shower of sparks an enormous pincered claw suddenly thrust itself under the raised shutter and began to scratch greedily away at the floor of the chamber. Then an angry, giant shape appeared in the rectangular opening, rearing and hissing in the semi-darkness...

Garron and Unstoffe crouched in the driving snow up on the tower roof, their numb bodies jarred by the tremors of the huge gong suspended somewhere below them. As soon as it was completely silent, Unstoffe pushed the hunk of raw, dripping meat over the edge of the trap. They listened as it thudded against the sides of the dark shaft and finally landed on the flagstones thirty metres below.

'Now the ladder,' Garron murmured, peering down into the blackness.

Unstoffe pulled a long rope-ladder from his sack and fixed the grapple-hook at one end onto the raised rim around the trap. 'We'd better give it a bit longer,' he whispered anxiously.

At that moment a raucous bellow erupted out of the shaft into their faces. Unstoffe all but pitched forward into the gaping hole in front of him. Garron seized his arm just in time and held him back. They cowered precariously on the edge of the trap, transfixed by the hoarse snarls and unearthly panting sounds echoing inside the shaft.

'You want me to go down *there*?' Unstoffe finally managed to gasp with chattering teeth and bone-dry throat.

'Stop worrying, my boy,' Garron rapped in a menacing tone, tightening his grip on Unstoffe's arm and tattered fur collar. 'We'll give it a few minutes.'

Soon the monstrous sounds began to subside, and

the only noise came from Unstoffe's rattling teeth and the relentless whine of the wind across the steppes.

'Right, down you go, my lad,' said Garron eagerly.

Unstoffe swallowed hard. 'But ... but it might have smelt us up here,' he stammered. 'It might not have touched the ... the meat ... It might just be waiting there ... for me.'

Garron eased the rope-ladder out of his friend's frozen hands and dropped it into the shaft. 'Trust me,' he hissed.

'Why ... why don't *you* go down,' Unstoffe suddenly demanded.

Garron patted his own vast fur-clad bulk. 'And if I got stuck in there?' he retorted. 'Then where would we be?'

Unstoffe was about to reply that at least he would know where he would be, but he thought better of it and said nothing.

'All our plans ...' Garron pleaded. 'It's all worked out; don't lose heart now, my boy.' He nearly added that at Unstoffe's age he had revelled in real danger, but he thought better of it and just gave a wink of encouragement instead.

Unstoffe did not move. Garron glanced up at the sky: the light was fading rapidly. 'Listen,' he said, 'that creature must be out for the count, it's as quiet as the grave down there ... In a manner of speaking,' he added with a forced chuckle. Then he pulled back his shaggy sleeve, exposing a small device resembling a wrist watch strapped to his forearm. 'And remember, we'll be in constant touch,' he said, patting Unstoffe's sleeve. Reluctantly, Unstoffe swung himself onto the swaying ladder and prepared to climb down into the shaft.

'You've got the Jethryk?' Garron whispered. Unstoffe nodded, pointing to the large leather pouch clipped to his belt. 'Guard it with your ... just remember its value, my lad,' Garron muttered, hastily correcting himself. Unstoffe grunted vaguely, and began to lower himself timidly into the narrow shaft. Within seconds he was swallowed up by the silent darkness.

When Unstoffe had almost reached the bottom of the ladder he paused and listened. From somewhere very close to him there came a deep, regular breathing which made the air in the shaft vibrate. He convinced himself that it was the sound of heavily drugged slumber, and gingerly crept down the last few rungs. To his relief the ladder just reached far enough down for him to have to jump only the last metre onto the flagstones. He landed without a sound and made towards the faint rectangle of light beneath the shutter leading into the Relic Chamber.

Suddenly a warm sour breath on the side of his face stopped him in his tracks. With racing heart he slowly turned his head and peered into the gloom. A colossal shape lay slumped against the far wall of the antechamber: a huge reptilian body covered in thick overlapping scales like armour-plate which slid back and forth over each other as the creature's vast flanks rose and fell. The long alligator head lay on one side, its half-open jaws bristling with razor-sharp and bloodstained teeth. A huge bone, picked clean and glistening, lay beside the monstrous lolling tongue.

Unstoffe shuddered. Then, reassured by the creature's rhythmical breathing, he pulled himself together and darted through into the Relic Chamber. Going straight to the cabinet he took a diamond glass-cutter and a large suction cup from his pouch. Licking his finger, he ran it round the rim of the rubber cup and then pressed it firmly against the centre of the main glass panel. It stuck fast. With careful practised movements he then began to score the edges of the panel with the diamond, just where they joined the solid wooden framework of the display case. As he worked he frequently paused to check the sound of breathing from the antechamber.

He knew that he had very little time . . .

*   *   *

Unstoffe eased the metre-square sheet of thick glass out of its frame and set it carefully down against the Relic Cabinet. Then he took from his pouch a jagged lump of crystalline rock the size of a grapefruit, and placed it among the clusters of precious stones and jewelled ornaments so that it was clearly visible but not too conspicuous. In the light from the single globe above the cabinet the jagged nugget glowed a deep indigo, shot with a honeycomb of filigree silver veins. Beads of sweat glistened on Unstoffe's crafty young face as he stepped back, and then leaned forward again to adjust the position of the hunk of Jethryk.

Suddenly a shrill bleeping made him jump with momentary terror. Swallowing hard, Unstoffe pulled back the sleeve of his fur tunic and hissed, 'What is it Garron?' into the tiny radio strapped to his wrist. Then he flicked a microswitch and put the device to his ear. For several seconds he heard nothing but the hiss of static.

' "Over" ... my boy. You have to say "over",' came Garron's faint voice through the crackling.

'Listen, I'm five metres away from a doped carnivore, so just tell me what you want,' Unstoffe muttered into the microphone.

'Oh I do wish I was there with you, my lad,' Garron crackled. 'It all sounds so exciting. Unfortunately, I've got to leave now.'

Unstoffe glanced uneasily towards the dark rectangle under the raised shutter: 'What? Leave me down *here*?' he croaked. 'Why?'

'The Graff Vynda Ka is arriving,' Garron explained patiently.

'The who?' Unstoffe croaked, the sweat oozing out of his scalp and trickling through his lank hair onto his scrawny neck.

'The Graff Vynda Ka—I have to go and meet him,' Garron enunciated slowly, as if he were speaking to a foreigner or an idiot.

'It's all right for some people,' Unstoffe retorted.

There was a brief mush of static, and then Garron's voice came hissing through. 'Look, this isn't going to be a doddle for *me* either,' he answered faintly. 'The Graff has just come down scarcely three kilometres outside the walls in a Levithia Class Stellacruiser on full retro-thrust. About as discreet as the Spithead Review.'

'The what?' Unstoffe whispered.

At that moment the massive creature in the antechamber shifted its heavy serrated tail against the flagstones with a harsh leathery rasping sound. Unstoffe's heart began to hammer against his scantily covered ribcage.

'We must stick to the plan now ...' Garron crackled urgently. 'Remember ... we mustn't be seen together ... not until all this is over and done with ...'

'But ... but where shall we meet?' Unstoffe muttered in a panicky stammer. He put his lips very close to the device fixed round his wrist. 'Here Garron, you wouldn't be thinking of double-crossing me would you?' he croaked suspiciously.

But there was no reply: only the hiss of static from the tiny speaker. Cold shudders flew along Unstoffe's spine as a raucous growling suddenly burst from the antechamber. Seizing the glass panel, he struggled to ease it back into position in the frame of the Relic Cabinet with violently trembling hands, while from the darkness the huge beast's breathing grew more and more alert ...

The Doctor stood motionless at the control console gloomily staring at the bleeping Locatormutor Core. Romanadvoratrelundar stood opposite, watching him with faint amusement.

'It's hopeless,' the Doctor eventually sighed, 'we'll never get on together.'

'Oh yes we will,' his new assistant said soothingly. 'You're just suffering from a transitory hypertoid syndrome with multi-encephalogical flaxions.'

'And what is that supposed to mean?' retorted the Doctor, still staring thoughtfully at the console.

'You're sulking,' came the smugly prompt reply. 'You will make a most interesting case-study for my thesis when I return to Gallifrey.'

The Doctor thrust his face towards the Vector Display in front of him. He watched it without speaking for several minutes. 'You won't be going back to Gallifrey ... not for quite some time,' he suddenly snapped, brushing rudely past his assistant and starting to re-programme the Helmic Orientator. 'For the moment you'll be going to the planet Ribos ...'

'Ribos?' Romanadvoratrelundar echoed. 'The Segment is there?'

The Doctor nodded. 'Assuming that this gadget of yours is working properly.' He gestured towards the Display: 'The vectors have not changed for the past hour.'

'Then we must go there at once,' Romanadvoratrelundar cried eagerly. The Doctor said nothing. 'Why should there be any delay?' she demanded.

The Doctor turned to her irritably. 'If the vectors were to alter while the TARDIS is in vortex ... we might lose the bearing on that Segment for ever,' he retorted.

'We must take a chance,' his assistant said firmly.

The Doctor spun round again. 'I'll make the decisions,' he snapped, with a murderous frown.

Quite unruffled, the young woman stared unblinkingly back at him. 'So, what do we do, Doctor?' she challenged.

The Doctor glared at her. 'We take a chance,' he muttered, giving the controls a sharp jerk with both hands. The TARDIS hummed and shuddered into life, and within seconds it had entered the hazardous and uncertain vortex mode ...

Pressing his conspicuous frame into the shadows as best

he could, Garron hurriedly made his way through the narrow twisting alleyways leading to the deserted outskirts of the city of Shurr. The sky was shot with the last pale glimmers of the planet's setting sun, reflecting its sinister greenish sheen in the treacherous patches of ice stretching between the rough stone walls and under the low archways. He had almost reached the neighbourhood of the city wall when, turning a sharp corner, he all but collided with two enormous angular figures coming in the opposite direction. Throwing himself sideways, he crammed his bulky fur-clad body between two thick buttresses and held his breath, the sweat bursting out all over his fleshy face despite the bitter cold.

Something sharp was thrust several times into his midriff. Then a pair of huge metal-gauntleted hands seized him by the collar and yanked him out of the niche. Garron found himself staring wild-eyed into a cylindrical steel mask, featureless except for narrow slits for the eyes and mouth. He hung there helplessly in the merciless grip of the huge armoured figure, struggling to regain his breath and desperately trying to speak. After a few seconds, he was thrust brutally aside into a deep snowdrift. He heard the steady crunch of marching boots approaching.

'Wel ... welcome to ... to Ribos ...' he stuttered, scrambling clumsily to his feet and stepping cautiously towards the two motionless Levithian Guards, his arms outstretched and with a forced smile of greeting on his clammy face.

Again he was shoved roughly aside. 'Back scum,' barked a harsh voice, muffled slightly by the heavy metal helmet. 'Make way for His Highness the Graff Vynda Ka ...' and at that moment, a squad of armoured guards swept round the corner.

Garron stepped forward again, drawing himself upright in a dignified manner. 'Indeed ... Indeed ... And I am here precisely in order to welcome His Highness to Ribos,' he announced in an affected tone.

The nearest guard immediately raised his slim, streamlined laser-spear to strike Garron a vicious blow across the face, but at the same instant a coldly authoritative voice sliced through the air.

'Garron ... ?' The squad abruptly halted. From the armour-plated ranks there emerged a shortish but athletic-looking young man dressed in richly decorated robes trimmed with fur, gleaming boots, and wearing a small but elaborate imperial crown on his sleek, close-cropped head.

Garron beamed at the aristocratic young man and made a low bow. 'Representing the Magellanic Mining Conglomerate, Highness,' he said humbly, flourishing a bundle of documents from the pouch at his belt. 'Allow me to present my credentials ...'

The Graff Vynda Ka waved the papers aside and stared at the fawning Garron with pale, chilling eyes, his thin nostrils curling with evident contempt. 'This is hardly a fitting reception,' he snapped after a short pause, during which Garron had squirmed uncomfortably, with nervous glances at the guards surrounding him.

Garron bowed again. 'I have comfortable quarters prepared for your Highness ...' he murmured, smiling effusively.

The Graff Vynda Ka gathered his cloak impatiently against the wind: 'Then let us delay no longer,' he said irritably, motioning Garron to show the way.

Garron hesitated, licking his fat lips nervously, and glancing at the huge armoured figures on each side of him. 'Highness ... my letter did stress the necessity for the utmost discretion,' he muttered with yet another bow. 'The natives on this planet are primitive people, easily intimidated ...'

'Well?' cried the Levithian Prince with a dangerous scowl.

'Your escort, Highness ...' Garron went on. 'There is a strict curfew in force, and it would be foolish to risk upsetting the ...'

'His Highness is never without his personal body-guard,' snapped a tall craggy-faced figure who carried his helmet under his arm.

'How I detest these covert operations ...' the young Prince murmured, studying Garron's obsequious, fish-eyed expression with an icy stare. He turned to the tall bare-headed Guard at his side. 'Send the squad back to the cruiser, Sholakh,' he ordered.

The Guard hesitated, staring at Garron through narrowed eyes. 'But, Highness ...' he began in an undertone.

The Graff Vynda Ka silenced him with a gesture and turned to Garron. 'Lead the way,' he ordered.

Garron glanced at the departing squad with a secret smile of triumphant satisfaction. Then, with an expansive sweep of the arm, he invited the Graff Vynda Ka and Sholakh to follow him.

Chapter 3

A Shaky Start

The column of elite Levithian Guards had only just disappeared over the brow of the low ridge bordering the outer wall of the city, when a pulsating whining and trumpeting sound tore through the freezing air, and a faint yellow light flashed in the shadows by the archway leading into the settlement. Beneath the pulsing light a blue box-like structure gradually took shape as the TARDIS materialised. For some time the image hovered fitfully in the air, fading and reappearing with an undulating groaning. At last it finally solidified with a shudder. The light stopped flashing and there was silence, except for the moan of the wind and a faint hiss of steam from the melted snow around the base of the Police Box.

After a few moments the door burst open and the Doctor stepped out. He glanced around and then took several deep breaths. 'Very fresh,' he murmured appreciatively. 'Faint smell of burning—but very refreshing.'

'It's *freezing*,' gasped Romanadvoratrelundar, hesitating in the doorway as she clasped her delicate white robe closer to her.

'We have obviously arrived in wintertime,' the Doctor exclaimed. 'Ribos orbits its sun elliptically, so the climate is one of extremes.'

Eagerly the Doctor scanned the low snow-covered ridge and the massive icicle-clustered walls of the city. 'Well, which way?' he demanded. His shivering companion fumbled with the bleeping Locatormutor Core. 'Do come along,' he cried impatiently.

'We must be quite close, Doctor,' she answered

28

through chattering teeth. 'It's a strong signal . . .'

'Which *way* then?' the Doctor repeated, setting off at a cracking pace across the slippery steppe towards the ridge.

'*That* way,' she called, pointing to the gateway in the city wall in the opposite direction. Abruptly the Doctor wheeled round and advanced rapidly towards the arch.

'Now I'm not expecting any trouble here,' he cried over his shoulder, 'but there are certain ground rules to be observed at all times . . .'

His unfortunate companion set off in pursuit, slithering and sliding all over the uneven surface, her thin robes flapping flimsily in the freezing wind.

'One: stay close to me. Two: do exactly as I tell you. Three: let me do all the talking . . .' the Doctor continued, disappearing under the archway. 'Oh, and by the way,' he said stopping and turning, 'your name. Too long. Sounds like a Siamese railway station. I'll call you Romana.'

Just then his struggling assistant caught up with him. 'I don't like Romana,' she objected, panting for breath.

The Doctor shrugged. 'It's either that or Fred,' he said.

'I prefer Fred,' she said after a brief pause.

'Good. Come on, Romana,' the Doctor cried, setting off once again. 'Four . . .' he went on, darting down a narrow side turning between high walls, 'always keep alert and watch out for the unexpectaaaaaaagh . . .'

The Doctor's cheerfully booming voice had turned abruptly into a strangled cry of shock and dismay which was swallowed up in the darkness ahead. Romana slowly advanced into the alleyway holding the bleeping Core out in front of her like a two-handed sword. In the gently pulsing glow of the Locatormutor, she saw the Doctor swinging helplessly in mid-air. He was completely enmeshed in a large net which was drawn tightly shut at the top and suspended from a rough wooden beam slung between the walls. He was upside down and doubled in two with his head jammed between his knees.

Romana suppressed a sudden urge to giggle. 'A primitive device to stop animals from straying into the city at night,' she suggested, keeping her face as straight as she could. 'There appears to be some kind of trigger mechanism set into the . . .'

'Well done,' the Doctor managed to mutter, 'I wondered if you'd spot that . . .' His face was almost purple. His long multicoloured scarf had become caught up in the crude rigging of the trap and had pulled tight around his throat. He glared at Romana, making incoherent and strangled sounds in frustration.

Finally the Doctor worked one hand free and was able to loosen the scarf a little. 'Now, my dear,' he whispered hoarsely in a supreme effort to keep calm, 'do you think you could turn your attention to getting me out of this thing . . . ?'

Having ushered the Graff Vynda Ka and his faithful commander, Sholakh, into their quarters in the Citadel, Garron set to work in an attempt to blow some life into the flickering logs piled in the iron grate.

'Unfortunately, Highness, you are not seeing the planet at its best just now,' he fawned, clumsily pumping a crude bellows and producing clouds of smoke in the windowless room. 'However, for someone in your exalted position Ribos would make an ideal second home during Sun Time.'

The Graff Vynda Ka shivered and stared disdainfully round the chamber, waving the smoke out of his face with white, well-manicured hands. 'Sun Time!' he snorted, 'once every eleven years . . . If I do purchase the planet it will not be my intention to spend much time here.'

'But there are so few unspoiled properties coming

onto the market at the moment, Highness,' Garron said affectedly, brushing his watering eyes with his sleeve. 'Shurr is the only city of any size; there are a few scattered settlements towards the Upper Pole—otherwise nothing.'

Sholakh had been marching about the fur-strewn flagstone floor, rubbing his numbed hands. 'The property grows less attractive every minute, Highness,' he muttered.

The Graff nodded and came over to warm himself at the modest blaze which Garron had succeeded in coaxing from the damp wood. He stared into the fire thoughtfully, the flames reflecting on his taut pale-skinned features.

'The inhabitants . . .' he suddenly demanded, '. . . are they aware of the existence of the Greater Cyrrhenic Empire? Do they know that their planet is protected by the Imperial Alliance?'

Garron hauled himself quickly to his feet, shaking his head firmly. 'They are brutish primitives, Highness,' he scoffed, 'they know nothing of other worlds . . . nothing at all.' He detected a flicker of renewed interest in the young Prince's pale blue eyes. 'Ribos is extremely well-positioned in the Galaxy—strategically speaking,' he murmured, leaning forward confidentially so that his face almost touched the Graff's.

The Prince's nostrils flared with undisguised contempt. 'You are keen to make a sale, Garron,' he said with a chilling smile.

Garron opened his pouch and took out a sheaf of papers. 'And you are keen to make a purchase, Highness,' he beamed. 'Otherwise you would not be here.'

'Not for the ten million opeks you are asking,' the Graff cried, turning brusquely away.

Carron shrugged. 'The Magellanic Mining Corporation set that valuation,' he replied. 'I am merely the agent . . .'

The Graff Vynda Ka pondered a moment. Then he

swung round and fixed Garron with a brooding stare. 'You are empowered to accept an offer?' he suddenly snapped.

Garron hastily lowered his eyes from the inside of the hollow shaft above the fire, where he had been gazing while the Graff had his back to him. 'A reasonable offer ... Yes, Highness,' he replied with a reassuring smile.

'What is wrong? What are you staring at?' Sholakh demanded suspiciously, going over to the fire.

Garron recovered himself instantly. He waved the sheaf of documents vigorously about in the air. 'I ... I was just looking to see if the chimney was obstructed,' he said soothingly. 'I do apologise for this smoke, Highness. I trust you will be comfortable here.'

Selecting several papers from the bundle, Garron led the way to the massive wooden table and spread them out with an impressive flourish. As he did so, one sheet slipped from his grasp and fluttered unnoticed to the floor.

'The documents of Title and Mortmain await your consideration, Highness,' Garron beamed, gesturing to the parchments as he bowed himself towards the door. 'Tomorrow it will be my pleasure to conduct you on a tour of the city: until then, may you rest in comfort, gentlemen.'

Leaving the Graff's quarters, Garron hurried a short distance through the maze of deserted stone passages which honeycombed the Citadel of Shurr, until he came to a deeply recessed doorway. Glancing quickly about to make sure that he was not being watched, he settled himself down in the shadows and huddled tightly into his furs. Then, with a devious grin, he put his wrist up to his ear and carefully adjusted the tiny switches on the communicator device strapped to it ...

'I think that he will accept six million opeks,' murmured the Graff Vynda Ka after rapidly scanning the documents Garron had placed on the table for his approval.

Sholakh had been staring at the paper which he had just picked up from under a chair. 'Look at this, Highness,' he breathed, 'the Conglomerate's Mineralogical Survey Report on Ribos—Garron must have dropped it by accident.'

The Graff glanced briefly at the document. Then he grabbed it from Sholakh and started to read it eagerly, a deep furrow appearing in the centre of his waxen forehead. After several minutes he looked up sharply. 'It is not possible ...' he cried. 'It must be a mistake.'

Sholakh looked inquiringly at his master, amazed by the sudden outburst.

'Point zero zero zero zero one per cent of planetary mass, Sholakh!' the Graff almost screamed, his eyes ablaze and his pale cheeks twitching. His trembling hands almost crumpled the paper as he held it up to re-read its incredible contents.

Sholakh stared at his master's face while he skimmed through the document a second time. 'What is it, Highness?' he murmured as the Graff slowly laid down the paper and rose to his feet.

'Jethryk!' the young Prince breathed hoarsely. 'Jethryk: the most valuable ... the most powerful element in the Galaxy.'

Sholakh frowned. 'As you say, a mistake, Highness,' he shrugged. 'Otherwise the Conglomerate would not be selling ...'

'Wait,' the Graff cried, seizing the documents from the table and feverishly shuffling through them. 'There was a condition ... Here ... "While relinquishing freehold in the planet Ribos ... in the constellation Skythra ... Magellanic Mining retains to itself sole right of exploitation in all mineral deposits ... in perpetuity" ... There is no mistake, Sholakh,' he cried his shrill voice tinged with hysteria. He began to stride agitatedly round and round the chamber, the firelight throwing his stalking shadow over the walls, and his voice rising gradually to fever pitch: 'Sholakh ... this is far beyond our wildest dreams ... Jethryk would guarantee success quicker than ever seemed possible ...'

Garron hugged himself with delight as he listened with mounting satisfaction to the Graff's excited voice crackling from the miniature radio on his wrist. 'Garron, old lad, you're a genius,' he chuckled, his plump features swollen in a huge grin. 'And just so long as that lily-livered butcher's boy, Unstoffe, doesn't do anything daft, we'll be ...'

'Oh dear. Has it stopped?' enquired a polite voice beside him.

Garron whipped round. The Doctor and Romana were standing in the passage, opposite the doorway where he was huddled. He stared at the two strangers for several seconds, completely at a loss. Then he recovered himself and screwed up his face in a bizarre smile. 'Oh na, thenk yer koyndly,' he growled. He glanced at the device strapped to his wrist. 'Faw a clock an awl's wewl myte ...' and with an exaggerated yawn he settled back into his voluminous furs and started to snore.

'Fascinating,' the Doctor whispered, frowning at the dozing figure slumped in the doorway.

'Obviously a ritual native greeting,' Romana murmured with a shrug. She was preoccupied with tuning the increasingly strong signal being emitted by the Locatormutor Core.

'In a bad Bermondsey accent?' the Doctor muttered doubtfully, shaking his head and moving off along the winding passage.

'Bermondsey?' Romana echoed blankly, catching up with him.

'Delightful suburb of London ... Earth,' the Doctor replied.

'Earth?' Romana exclaimed. 'There cannot be any

34

Earth aliens here on Ribos, Doctor.' Checking the signal again, she pointed the way through a wide arch decorated with crude carvings.

'Perhaps he's a cricket scout,' the Doctor grinned, disappearing down a steep flight of broad stone steps, worn away as if by the feet of generations of pilgrims. 'They desperately need a good opening bat just now . . .'

'What do you mean?' Romana demanded, following the Doctor down into the semi-darkness.

'Do keep up,' the Doctor called over his shoulder. 'Remember Rule One . . .'

At the bottom of the long flight of dark, winding steps the Doctor and Romana found themselves in an arched lobby with passages leading off in all directions. Facing them was a pair of massive wooden doors secured by a stout iron bar locked into place. In the alcove beside the doors an enormous Shrieve Guard was sound asleep huddled in his uniform of mouldy furs and plaited leather, his pike leaning against the wall next to him.

'In there, Doctor,' Romana said, nodding towards the doors. 'The signal is almost at optimum focus.'

The Doctor frowned at her and put his finger to his lips. Quickly, he examined the locks securing the iron bar. 'Did the Academy teach you anything about locks?' he whispered.

Romana shook her head. 'There was no time for such elementary activities,' she retorted.

'Then how are we going to get in?' the Doctor asked with a worried look.

'That is not my problem. I am only here as your assistant,' Romana replied smugly.

'In that case you take care of the sentry while I sort out this little difficulty,' the Doctor grinned, taking out an enormous pair of tweezers and setting to work. After a few minutes there was a soft click, and the Doctor swung the bar through ninety degrees and pushed one of the doors carefully open.

'After you, my dear,' he whispered.

As they entered the dimly-lit Relic Chamber the Doctor gently pushed the massive door to behind him. Neither he nor Romana noticed the quiet whirring and clicking as the iron bar slowly swung back into place, locking the doors from the outside.

Holding the Core out in front of her, Romana approached the Relic Cabinet. The Core was now emitting a continuous signal and glowing steadily.

'The Segment must be something in here, Doctor,' she said.

'Well of course it must,' the Doctor muttered, joining her. He scanned the contents of the display-case closely. 'We'll be very unpopular if we get caught tampering with the Crown Jewels—so we'd better identify the Segment, convert it and depart before the natives wake up.' He thrust out a large hand: 'Hammer!'

Romana cast her eyes upwards in despair. 'If we shatter the glass, the guard will wake up,' she explained, as if speaking to a young child.

'Just as well,' the Doctor retorted, feeling carefully round the frame of the cabinet. 'Sleeping on duty is a capital offence.'

Romana looked daggers at the Doctor's back. 'You realise that your sarcasms are merely adjustive stress reactions,' she said loftily.

'You are quite right. I really must see a doctor about it,' the Doctor replied. He spun round sharply. 'Haven't you brought anything except that gadget you keep waving?' he snapped. 'For goodness' sake switch it off. It's getting on my nerves.'

With that the Doctor wriggled underneath the cabinet. Lying on his back in the cramped space he inspected the base of the display. Then he extracted an enormous old-fashioned corkscrew from his pocket and started poking about on the underside of the wooden structure.

Romana walked impatiently around the chamber,

36

glancing from time to time to see what progress the Doctor was making.

'Why are you taking so much time?' she demanded at last with a sigh of exasperation. The Doctor muttered an inaudible reply. With a bored shrug Romana wandered over to the rectangular opening in the wall of the chamber and peered into the darkness beyond...

The Graff Vynda Ka was pacing around his lodging like a caged panther, clutching the Mineralogical Survey Report in white-knuckled hands.

'Rest, Sholakh?' he hissed. 'I shall not rest for one single moment until I have won back the Levithian throne which is mine—mine by right.'

'Indeed, Highness,' his faithful military Commander nodded wearily, 'Ribos would be an ideal forward base in our campaign. But to give the planet the necessary technology ... to train the primitives and create a force capable of reconquering our Levithian homeland—all this could take centuries.'

The Graff brandished the Survey Document. 'You are faithful and brave, Sholakh, but you have no *imagination*,' he murmured. 'Providence has put into my hand a weapon already forged. If we can locate and mine the Jethryk we shall have the means to raise a vast force of conquering mercenaries from outside the Alliance.' He grasped Sholakh by the shoulder and fixed him with his burning, fanatical gaze: 'Think of it, Sholakh—in ten years we could return in triumph, our unjust exile at an end ...'

For a few moments Sholakh shared his master's vision. Then he gently disengaged himself and went over to the fire. 'Highness, we are not experts,' he protested quietly. 'Even if there is a vein of Jethryk on Ribos—we might search for ever and still not find it.'

The Graff Vynda Ka stared at his Commander with the faintest trace of scorn curling his upper lip. He held up the document, his hands trembling with anticipation and excitement. 'You forget, Sholakh ...' he muttered through clenched teeth. 'Experts can be bought easily enough.'

On the flat rooftop of the Citadel Tower, high above the Relic Chamber, a young Shrieve Guard dumped a large skin sack and a curious serpentine horn beside the trap. With a yawn, he knocked back the locking tabs and grasped the thick iron plate as if it were a featherweight.

'Top of the day, my friend,' hailed a sudden voice beside him.

The Shrieve dropped the plate with a crash and leaped up. Unstoffe quailed at the huge figure looming over him, and was instantly yanked bodily from the flagstones and held by the collar like a sack. Struggling for breath, he managed to pull a small skin bottle from his furs and uncork it. 'Fancy a drop?' he gasped, trying desperately to smile. He held the flask in front of the hard, angular face of the young Guard who was staring suspiciously at him. 'It ... it works wonders ... against the cold ...' Unstoffe stammered encouragingly, '... when I'm out in ... in the tundra every day at first ... light ... setting my traps ...'

The Shrieve glanced warily at the skin bottle. Then he grinned broadly. 'You're a trapper,' he grunted, letting his victim drop and seizing the flask in his huge hand.

Unstoffe nodded eagerly, thankful to have escaped being strangled and flung over the parapet. Loosening his collar, he gratefully gulped the freezing air.

The Guard took a swig from the flask and smacked his lips approvingly. 'Did you make this yourself?' he grinned, blinking several times and taking a few deep breaths.

Unstoffe nodded. 'Have another ...' he suggested slyly.

With a chuckle, the young Shrieve took several huge mouthfuls. His eyes began to water and sweat broke out over his rock-like features as he clumsily handed back the flask to the beady-eyed Unstoffe. 'Any more of th ... that and I'll not have b ... breath to call the Sh ... Shriven ... venzale in for its feed ...' he stuttered, slumping to his knees and straining to move the trap aside.

'Allow me,' Unstoffe cried, bending to help. Together they slid the trap open.

The Shrieve rubbed his bleary eyes and peered into the shaft. 'Is the b-beast there ... I can't see any ...' Swaying unsteadily, he suddenly keeled over onto his side.

At once Unstoffe grabbed the twisted brass horn and directed it into the dark shaft below the trap. He blew a long rasping blast that echoed in the depths of the tower for several seconds. Then he turned to the motionless bulk of the unconscious young Guard. Above the tower, the sky was already streaked with pale green light which increased every minute. He would have to work very quickly indeed ...

Romana flinched away from the dark opening beneath the shutter as the ear-splitting blast of the horn was amplified in the antechamber. 'Whatever was that?' she gasped when the echoes had subsided.

'End of the curfew no doubt,' came the Doctor's muffled reply from under the Relic Cabinet.

Her curiosity aroused, Romana crept slowly back to the rectangular hole and ventured through. As her eyes grew accustomed to the gloom, she noticed the faint greenish glimmer coming from the shaft in the ceiling of the antechamber. As she stood there looking up, she gradually became aware of a very slow rhythmic breathing reverberating around her. Then she heard something move in the shadows as the tail of the waking Shrivenzale twitched. Unable to move,

Romana held her breath and listened, screwing up her eyes in a vain attempt to penetrate the darkness surrounding her.

As the Shrivenzale began to stir, its breathing changed to a throaty growl and a harsh grating sound suddenly tore through the darkness as its scaly underbelly dragged against the floor. Romana stared wildly about, desperately trying to discover what was happening. Suddenly she had a terrifying glimpse of razor-sharp teeth and needle-sharp claws. Panic-stricken she spun round but saw to her horror that the shutter had begun to descend, cutting off her escape into the Relic Chamber. Half paralysed with panic, she forced herself to glance round once more. The beast's scales squeaked shrilly against each other as it shook itself into consciousness. There was a nightmarish snorting as the monster scented live prey within its grasp.

Her voice frozen in her throat, Romana flung herself round; but before she could dive to safety through the rapidly narrowing space under the stone shutter, she was caught as the Shrivenzale savagely flicked its massive serrated tail, and hurled her violently across the antechamber. For several seconds Romana lay stunned at the foot of the wall, while the Shrivenzale dragged its greedily panting bulk towards her.

Half-dazed, she saw that the shutter was barely a metre from the flagstones. With a supreme effort she scrambled to her feet and struggled frantically over to the dimly lit gap. Grasping the lower edge of the falling block, she tried vainly to check its descent. 'Doctor ...' she gasped, as she felt the beast's hot, sour breath on her back. 'Doctor ... please ...'

Suddenly the monstrous breathing paused and Romana whipped round, her fingers slipping helplessly from the sharp slab. Two enormous lizard-like eyes blinked at her hungrily, and then with renewed savagery the Shrivenzale clawed at the floor, sending up showers of crackling sparks all around her.

At that moment the Doctor's head appeared through the gap by Romana's feet. He braced his shoulders under the shutter and struggled to stop it descending the last fifty centimetres to the flagstones. 'Quick ... Romana ... Quick ...' he gasped as the weight of the huge slab began to crush him like a blunt but deadly guillotine.

Romana threw herself flat and just managed to roll through the gap into the Relic Chamber before the Shrivenzale could get its slicing claws into her body. She stared helplessly as the shutter continued its remorseless fall with the Doctor spreadeagled underneath it ...

In the low-arched lobby outside the Sacred Relic Chamber, the two Shrieves manning the winch turned to the Captain of the Shrievalty in bewilderment: 'Captain, the shutter will not close,' one of them growled.

'There must be some obstruction,' the Captain frowned. 'Take it up again—it could be the Shrivenzale.' As he spoke, the beast's roars reverberated through the Citadel with increased fury.

Straining at the winch, the two guards glanced at each other apprehensively.

'Now lower again,' the Captain ordered, shouting to make himself heard. This time the winch-handle turned freely until it reached its 'closed' position.

The Captain unclipped the large key-ring from his belt. 'It must have been the beast,' he shrugged, going over to the massive doors of the Sacred Chamber. 'I hope it is not injured.'

Chapter 4

Double Dealings

Romana clung tightly to the Doctor's arms as they watched the stone slab sink into its shallow groove in the floor, finally sealing the Shrivenzale in its lair beneath the tower.

'How did you *do* that, Doctor?' she eventually managed to ask, as the Doctor rolled his shoulders slowly back and forth to ease the pain.

'Oh, just a little Tibetan breathing exercise I picked up,' the Doctor said shrugging. Then he winced at the sudden sharp cramps in his chest. 'It's amazing what one can do with a little practice.'

Romana could not take her eyes away from the shutter. 'I never imagined ... are there many ... creatures ... like that in the other worlds?' she asked quietly.

'Oh, no end of them,' the Doctor grinned, flailing his arms briskly like windmill sails to restore the circulation.

At that moment Romana stiffened. 'There's someone coming,' she murmured.

The Doctor grabbed her by the arm and led her quickly over to the doors: 'This is no time for physical jerks, you know,' he whispered. 'Remember Rule Four ...' Pushing Romana to one side of the wide doorway, he dodged across to the other side and pressed himself flat against the wall, trying to hear what was happening in the lobby outside.

'Did you get the Segment?' Romana mouthed.

For a moment the Doctor simply stared at his assistant in disbelief. Then he shook his head.

42

'Why not? You had plenty of time,' Romana whispered, exasperated.

The Doctor glared murderously. Just in time he stopped himself from shouting a withering reply. 'I happened to get rather caught up in a little problem *you* were having—if you remember,' he mouthed furiously.

Just then there was a clattering and whirring of locks and both doors swung slowly open. The Doctor and Romana were hidden from view as the Captain entered, followed by his Shrieves. The Guards formed a semi-circle and everyone bowed solemnly to the glittering treasures.

'We give thanks for the new Dawn,' intoned the Captain.

'We give thanks,' the Guards repeated.

'And for the retreat of the Powers of Darkness,' concluded the Captain, raising his ceremonial mace.

'We give thanks,' the Shrieves again repeated. Then they proceded to light the globes suspended around the chamber using smoking tapers fixed to long poles. The Captain briefly glanced at the Relics, and then went over to examine the tightly closed shutter.

The Doctor peered cautiously round the edge of the door. 'If we're caught we'll either be boiled in oil or fed to that thing for breakfast,' he murmured to himself, 'so just stay where you are and keep quiet, madam...'

Just then Garron swept into the chamber alone. He bowed low before the Relic Cabinet, with a quick glance to see that the nugget of Jethryk was safely in place. 'Good lad, Unstoffe,' he breathed. 'I give thanks for a safe journey ...' he went on in an affected voice as the Captain came over to him and looked his stout, fur-clad figure suspiciously up and down.

'Where are you from?' the Captain demanded.

'I am from the North sir ... from the Upper Pole. Just arrived,' Garron beamed, handing the Captain a document bearing a number of impressive seals. 'This pass authorises myself and my colleagues to enter and leave the noble city of Shurr without let or hindrance.'

The Doctor listened intently behind the thick door. 'Sounds more like a Knightsbridge accent all of a sudden,' he murmured, recognising Garron from their encounter in the passage earlier.

The Captain looked carefully at the seals. 'From the Upper Pole.' He frowned. 'Purpose of your journey?'

'Trade Captain—I am a merchant,' Garron explained, with a condescending little bow. 'The Outer Settlements need fresh supplies.'

'And you need fat profits,' the Captain retorted.

Garron gave a cautionary wave of the hand. 'Believe me, it is no pleasure crossing the tundra during the Ice Time, with a sleigh-train of valuable cargo—prey to all the wild creatures and torn by that wind,' he murmured, leaning confidentially towards the Captain. 'And some of those crevasses are several kilometres deep ...' Garron let the effect of his words sink in a moment, then he shrugged modestly. 'Of course I am only in a small line of business myself, but I have a colleague who is carrying a substantial sum in excess of ...' and he whispered closely in the Captain's ear.

'A million gold ...' the Captain breathed incredulously.

'Perhaps more,' Garron nodded, his finger to his lips.

The Captain stared at Garron with growing respect. 'If a word of this was to get out ...' he murmured, glancing round at the busily-occupied Shrieves.

Garron nodded vigorously. 'We might all be murdered in our beds—there's so much lawlessness about.' He ventured a few steps towards the Relic Cabinet. 'My colleague is anxious to find a safe depository for his funds—just for the next day or so, and he is willing to pay a generous commission in return,' Garron went on as the Captain joined him. Again he leaned confidingly towards the silent Shrieve. 'And it occurs to me, Captain,' he continued in a low voice, 'that nowhere in the city is more secure than this Relic Cabinet, so closely guarded as it is by the Shrivenzale, and by yourself and your excellent Shrieves.'

Garron wandered casually around the cabinet for a few moments, admiring the Sacred Relics and nodding graciously to the Guards. Then he stopped beside the Captain: 'What do you say?' he murmured. 'A commission of one thousand gold opeks was mentioned, I believe ...'

The Captain stared at Garron in shocked amazement. Then he shook his head violently. 'The Relic Cabinet is a sacred place,' he protested. 'It is forbidden on pain of death to ...'

'Oh, I quite understand,' Garron interrupted, waving his hands as if dismissing the subject and turning to leave. 'My apologies, Captain—I am forgetting myself,' he said humbly, and made towards the door.

The Captain followed after a moment's thought and stopped Garron in the entrance. 'Of course ... a contribution of one thousand opeks to the Sacred Funds would be most ...' he began.

Garron swung round with a smile: 'Did I say one thousand? Oh, no, no, no,' he murmured apologetically, 'ten thousand, my dear Captain ... ten thousand.'

The Shrieve's eyes widened and he swallowed visibly. 'You said just for two or three days ... ?' he asked in an undertone.

Garron nodded. 'Maybe less,' he said.

The Captain spoke briefly in Garron's ear, and then went over to supervise his Guards.

'I am deeply, deeply obliged, Captain,' Garron beamed. 'I shall go at once and inform my colleague.' With that, he retreated through the doorway, bowing low and elaborately towards the Relics.

At once the Doctor darted from his hiding place and bustled Romana out of the chamber, his hand clapped firmly over his startled assistant's mouth. As they hurried up the worn steps Romana managed to free herself, not without some difficulty.

'What now?' she demanded. 'How are we going to remove the Segment from the cabinet?'

'We aren't just for the moment,' the Doctor muttered, pushing her unceremoniously into an alcove while some citizens passed them on their way to make obeisance to the Relics.

'You seem very unconcerned, Doctor,' Romana murmured reproachfully. 'We do have an assignment to carry out, you know.'

'Our first job is to follow our "merchant from the north",' the Doctor snapped, setting off again as soon as the way was clear.

Reluctantly, Romana tagged along as the Doctor darted in and out of alcoves and doorways, carefully shadowing Garron as he waddled breathlessly through the maze of passageways. 'We are wasting valuable time, Doctor,' she protested. 'We should ignore this ... this insignificant stranger.'

The Doctor suddenly stopped dead in his tracks, whirled round and seized Romana's arm. 'What if *he's* after the Segment, too?' he retorted. 'You hadn't thought of that had you, my dear?' he added with a superior smile, hurrying on again.

Romana looked very startled. 'If he is, then he must at all costs be prevented,' she said in an outraged voice, catching up and clutching at the Doctor's sleeve.

The Doctor smiled in obvious amusement at his assistant's frustration. 'Oh, I don't know,' he said, 'it could save us a great deal of trouble if our merchant friend has devised an efficient method of removing the Segment from the cabinet ...'

Before Romana could reply, the Doctor pulled her sideways into a deep alcove beneath a low arch. Ahead of them, Garron had stopped in front of a door. After looking furtively up and down the apparently deserted passage, he knocked softly and was immediately admitted.

46

'Unless, of course, he's an agent of the Black Guardian,' the Doctor murmured, peering round the edge of the alcove. 'Oh dear ...' he went on, putting a hand over his mouth, 'you're not supposed to know about that, are you?'

Trying very hard to keep calm, Romana stood face to face with the Doctor in the confined space and spoke through clenched teeth: 'Doctor, I do wish you would stop treating me like a child.'

'But my dear—you *are* a child,' the Doctor grinned. 'On the other hand, he might be just a petty swindler; we'll simply have to wait and see.' Winding his long scarf around his neck against the bitter cold, the Doctor settled himself to wait for Garron's reappearance. 'Don't worry,' he said gently, giving Romana's arm a squeeze of reassurance, 'you'll soon learn the ropes. Fascinating, isn't it?'

As he entered the Graff Vynda Ka's quarters, Garron put on his air of polite humility. He went over to give the dying fire a boost with the bellows, and asked if the Graff had passed a comfortable night.

'I have slept in worse places,' the Levithian Prince replied with a grimace of disgust, 'but the Cyrrhenic Allies forgot the sacrifices I made in their service easily enough.' Angrily he shook the dust out of his robe and fixed Garron with blazing eyes. 'I returned battle-scarred from their campaigns to find myself deposed and my half-brother on the Levithian Throne. Where was the Alliance then?' he cried.

Garron was completely taken aback by the Graff's hysterical outburst. He shook his head and tut-tutted and clasped and unclasped his podgy white hands.

Pale-faced and violently trembling, the Graff stared into the fire. 'Not a single hand was raised in my support ...' he hissed.

Sholakh came forward from the shadows, his ever-watchful eye on Garron's artful face. 'Do not dwell on the past, Highness,' he murmured. 'We must prepare for the future now.'

Gradually the Graff Vynda Ka calmed himself. 'Good advice, as ever, my faithful Sholakh,' he nodded. Suddenly he strode to the table. Snatching a handful of papers, he thrust them directly under Garron's misshapen nose. 'This preposterous figure of ten million opeks ...' he cried.

'It ... it is negotiable, Highness ...' Garron mumbled.

The Graff thrust his cruel, chiselled features into Garron's sweating, waxen face. 'Tell me, Garron,' he snarled, 'why is the Conglomerate selling the planet if it intends to keep the mineral exploitation rights for itself—for ever?'

Garron stared back at the young Prince like a hypnotised animal. 'Oh, some temporary shortage of cash perhaps ...' he smiled uncomfortably, dabbing at his temples with a grubby handkerchief. 'The condition is a common one in such deals, Highness ...'

Sensing that his back was against a wall, Garron launched into an elaborate explanation of how Ribos was still only a Grade Three Planet with protected inhabitants, and that mining would not be possible until it had achieved Grade Two status. That, he concluded, would not happen for hundreds of years.

The Graff Vynda Ka continued to stare impassively at him. The fire was beginning to scorch the back of Garron's legs, and he tried to move a step or two, but Sholakh and the Graf blocked his way.

'None of this can possibly affect your Highness's enjoyment of the property,' Garron continued desperately.

'Enjoyment?' the young Prince suddenly burst out.

Taking a deep breath, Garron pushed gently past them. 'Perhaps when I have shown your Highness some of the more attractive features of the planet?' Garron pleaded. 'May I suggest that we begin by paying our respects to the Sacred Relics of Ribos?' and with that, he led the way towards the door.

Meanwhile the Doctor had drawn aside a heavy skin drape hung across the back of the arched alcove where he and Romana were concealed, and was looking out over a large colonnaded square over which hung a dense pall of smoke. Round the sides of the square were clustered dozens of ramshackle lean-to hovels, and crowds of ragged, fur-clad figures were milling about in the shadows.

'Fascinating, isn't it?' the Doctor murmured. 'No doubt fuel is rationed here and so the inhabitants are forced to ...'

Romana exploded in sheer frustration. 'Doctor, will you please try to keep your attention on the vital assignment with which we have been entrusted?' she cried.

The Doctor whipped off his hat and stuffed it over Romana's face. Voices were approaching along the passage. With a single sweep of the arm, he shoved her into the narrow space between the hide curtain and the small window opening. Seconds later the unsuspecting Garron passed by, conducting the Graff and Sholakh towards the Relic Chamber.

'For example, the great Crown of Ribos—most interesting Highness ...' Garron was holding forth pompously as they strode by without a glance. 'Almost nine thousand years old. The natives believe that whoever wears it has the power to ...'

'Call up the sun again at the end of each Ice Time.' The Doctor completed Garron's sentence under his breath as the trio passed out of earshot. 'Fascinating superstition, don't you think?' he remarked, uncovering Romana's face which was almost purple with indignation.

'Doctor, it must be the Crown,' she said decisively. 'The Segment must be disguised in the form of the Crown of Ribos.'

The Doctor silenced her with a reproving look. 'Never, never jump to conclusions like that,' he warned. 'They can lead you up the garden path ... and stop you seeing the wood for the trees.'

Romana's finely arched eyebrows rose higher still, and her well-shaped chin stuck out even further as she retorted: 'Such figures of speech betray a serious lack of logico-cognitive discipline, Doctor.'

The Doctor blinked. Then he clutched at his belly as if he had just been run through with a sword. Finally he shook his head violently from side to side as if recovering from a knockout blow. 'I really cannot stand here indulging in verbal fisticuffs with *you*,' he exclaimed. 'I have an assignment to complete.'

With that, he flung aside the drape and shot off down the passageway in the direction of the Relic Chamber.

In the Sacred Chamber, Garron continued his elaborate salesman's patter: 'Observe the workmanship, Highness, the honest peasant artistry achieved with nothing but the crudest implements. What treasures lie in this holy cabinet ...'

Sholakh was motionless in front of the display, his gaze fixed on the blue and silver nugget of Jethryk. 'Highness,' he breathed. 'Highness, look ...'

Nodding and faintly smiling in Garron's direction, the Graff Vynda Ka murmured out of the side of his mouth: 'I have seen it, Sholakh. There can be no mistaking it.'

But Garron had observed the effect of the nugget with carefully concealed satisfaction. Immediately he started to move round the cabinet. 'Now notice over here the ...'

The Graff raised his heavily gloved hand. 'This silver-blue stone here—it is called Jethryk, is it not?' he enquired casually.

Garron went through the motions of peering at the nugget. 'I really have no idea, Highness,' he said, shrugging. 'It's pretty though, whatever it is. Now over here, Highness, we see ...'

The Graff moved closer to the cabinet. 'Perhaps one of the attendants could enlighten us,' he suggested, watching Garron constantly.

Reluctantly Garron turned to the nearest Shrieve, who was dressed in an extremely ill-fitting assemblage of skins, furs and plaited leather. 'I say, fellow,' he shouted haughtily. 'That blue stone there—what is it?'

The Shrieve raised his head. It was Unstoffe. Garron was flabbergasted. He took several seconds to conquer his shock and surprise, glaring at Unstoffe with his back to the others.

At that moment the Doctor and Romana entered the Relic Chamber unobserved. They bowed briefly to the Sacred Cabinet and then lingered unobtrusively in the background.

'What is the stone called, fellow?' Garron demanded again, his voice cracking and his puffy features growing almost apoplectic with outrage.

The Shrieve respectfully touched his forelock and shuffled forward. 'That be what we calls Skrynge Stone, sir,' he mumbled. 'If you hangs a bit round your neck, sir, you won't never suffer from the skrynges, no matter how cold it be ...'

For some time Garron could only stare at his grinning young associate in silent disbelief. Then he recovered himself enough to say that no doubt the stone was pretty common on the planet.

Unstoffe said nothing.

Garron glanced at the Graff Vynda Ka and Sholakh and then turned back to the Shrieve with a stirring motion of his podgy hands. 'There's a lot of it about, I suppose,' he muttered, grimacing suggestively.

'Oh no, sir,' Unstoffe suddenly said. 'The secret of the mines was lost.'

The Graff Vynda Ka swept towards Unstoffe, his forehead etched with a deep frown: 'Secret ... Lost ...?' he murmured threateningly.

Garron turned away, flushed with anger and dismay.

'One Ice Time, sir, a glacier come and destroyed

51

the mine,' Unstoffe explained. 'Ever since they been searching an' asearching—but they'll never find it, sir ... they'll never find it.'

The Graff glanced at Sholakh. 'Even if the mine is buried, its approximate location must be known,' he snapped.

Unstoffe shrugged and said nothing.

Garron turned to the Levithian Prince with a scornful laugh. 'Pay no attention to these fairy tales, Highness,' he cried.

Unstoffe rapped the flagstones with his pike. 'My own poor father spent his life seeking that mine, and I reckon as how he must have found it just before he died,' he said solemnly.

Garron had meanwhile edged closer to his reckless young friend. Suddenly he trod heavily on Unstoffe's foot.

'This is sheer fantasy, Highness,' Sholakh scoffed.

The Graff's cold blue eyes narrowed to dangerously glinting slits. 'No one jests with *me*, Sholakh. No one,' he hissed.

Quite unabashed, Unstoffe pushed past Garron and went right up to the Graff Vynda Ka. 'That there nugget was found on my poor father's frozen body, sir, wrapped up in this,' he said holding out a ragged skin parchment.

The Graff and Sholakh carefully scanned the mouldy, faded sketch. 'A crude map,' the Graff breathed, eagerly reaching out to take the parchment, his eyes widening in anticipation.

'Maybe sir ... maybe ...' Unstoffe grinned, quickly thrusting the disintegrating sketch into his furs. A shadow of fury passed over the Levithian Prince's face as he nodded significantly to Sholakh.

Just then a group of Shrieve Guards entered the chamber to relieve those on duty.

'Change of the Watch,' Unstoffe said, bowing briefly to the Graff and to the boggle-eyed Garron before tagging on to the departing picket. As he left, he managed to wink at Garron, unseen by the others.

'What a fascinating story. My friend and I could not help overhearing,' the Doctor said amiably, appearing round the corner of the Relic Cabinet. 'It had the ring of truth about it, don't you think?' he added, turning to Romana.

She smiled ironically. 'The fellow certainly had an honest, open face,' she agreed.

Overcoming his anger and frustration with Unstoffe, Garron gave the Doctor a brazen look. 'Do you live in Shurr?' he enquired politely in his most polished manner.

The Doctor grinned broadly. 'No. We are from the Norff,' he replied, in a mixture of East End and Knightsbridge accents.

The Graff Vynda Ka stirred impatiently. 'Garron, we should be moving on,' he rapped.

When they had gone, the Doctor went over and peered into the cabinet. 'Fascinating,' he muttered. 'That's quite the biggest piece of Jethryk I have ever seen. I wonder if our multilingual friend, Garron, is aware of its value?' He frowned, surreptitiously examining the re-sealed edge of the glass panel which Unstoffe had replaced earlier. 'Found in a dead man's pocket ... a lost mine ... a faded map ...' he murmured doubtfully to himself.

Suddenly the Doctor put his mouth close to Romana's ear. 'Someone has broken into this cabinet ... and recently,' he whispered, pointing to the edge of the panel.

Romana instantly drew the Locatormutor Core from under her cloak. 'We must not lose track of the Segment, Doctor,' she breathed. 'If it has been taken there is no time to ...'

'Nor is this the time to get ourselves turned into glue,' the Doctor interrupted quietly, noticing that one of the Shrieve Guards was eyeing them suspiciously, 'so kindly put that infernal gadget away ...'

'Eight million opeks, my final offer, Garron,' the Graff Vynda Ka cried, turning his back contemptuously and staring into the fire—his thoughts fixed on the future.

Garron nodded resignedly. 'I shall have to go to Skythros and contact the Magellanic Conglomerate by hypercable, Highness,' he said.

'That will take at least a month!' Sholakh protested.

'And, of course, my clients will require a deposit ...' Garron went on, ignoring Sholakh. 'Say two million opeks.'

'A deposit?' Sholakh spat out the word incredulously. 'His Highness is a Prince of the Greater Cyrrhenic Empire. His word is his bond.'

A sharp, high-pitched whine suddenly burst momentarily through the chamber. Garron whipped round. Seated at the table, Sholakh was holding his laser-spear and checking its charging circuits connected to the Thermite unit attached to his belt. The Levithian Commander's steely eyes bore relentlessly into his. Garron started to sweat as he searched desperately for words to calm the situation.

'One million opeks,' the Graff suddenly rapped without turning round.

Garron beamed with relief, his hands clasping and unclasping nervously over his large belly. 'I am sure that a deposit of one million will be entirely acceptable to my clients, Highness,' he said, licking his dry lips.

Sholakh was gaping at his master in shocked amazement. 'Highness, if this creature gets his hands on a million opeks and is allowed to leave Ribos—what guarantee do we have?'

'A prudent question, Highness,' Garron interrupted, 'and I can set your mind entirely at rest: the deposit money will be lodged here in Shurr under the protection of the Captain of the Shrievalty, guarded night and day.'

Unknown to Garron, the Graff had turned his gaze upward and was at that moment staring at something jammed into a soot-filled crevice inside the chimney shaft. He considered a moment. Then, still without turning round, he instructed Sholakh to return to the Stellacruiser and fetch the money for the deposit.

When Sholakh protested strongly, the Graff raised his hand sharply. Sholakh hesitated, then bowed, picked up his helmet and went to the door, his eyes constantly on Garron's.

'I will accompany you to the City Wall,' Garron proposed with a gracious smile.

As soon as he was alone, the Graff Vynda Ka slipped off one of his gauntlets, reached carefully up into the blackened chimney and took down a small metal object about the size and shape of a matchbox. He studied it with a grim stare, his cheek twitching in rapid spasms and his jaw clenched like a sprung trap. 'No one crosses the Graff Vynda Ka ...' he muttered, muffling the device in his sinewy hand. 'No one.'

Chapter 5

Arrest and Capture

Romana stood staring angrily at the mass of glittering treasures in the Relic Cabinet. Her impatience with the Doctor was rapidly approaching the limits of endurance. He was pacing the flagstones of the chamber with his chin sunk onto his chest, deep in thought. He moved from the cabinet to the door, then back to the cabinet, then across to the shutter in the far wall and finally back to the cabinet—as if in some kind of trance. But whenever he passed one of the Shrieve Guards he looked up with an affable smile and a nod.

At last Romana could stand it no longer. 'What is happening?' she demanded in a furious whisper, trying hard to keep up with the Doctor's erratic steps across the huge chequered floor.

'A Triple Alpha Graduate surely does not need to have the situation explained,' he muttered. 'You have all the facts: examine them.'

Romana folded her arms as if to stop herself provoking a showdown. 'Doctor, I refuse to give way to your obvious attempts to trigger an inadequacy syndrome in my behaviour,' she said with forced calmness.

'Knight to Queen's Bishop Three ...' the Doctor replied, glancing down at his feet which were planted widely and awkwardly apart on the flagstones, and then glancing up at the vaulted roof above them.

'We are not making any progress at all ...' Romana pleaded.

The Doctor turned to face her. 'I agree—we need some fresh air at once,' he cried, and with a hasty bow towards the Relics, he marched straight out of the chamber.

Romana caught up with him at the foot of the steps outside. '*Now* where?' she asked plaintively.

'Up onto the roof, my dear,' the Doctor said, bounding up three steps at a time. 'I'm told there's a staggering view ...'

The sky was a lurid pattern of green streaks and orange spirals as the Doctor and Romana huddled over the trap, struggling to shift the iron plate aside. Suddenly, above the tortured moan of the wind, a monstrous bellow of rage and hunger rose from the shaft and echoed in the eerie light around them.

'Yes, this is the back door all right,' the Doctor said, peering into the darkness below. 'They must have used a rope ladder.'

'Who?' Romana cried impatiently.

'Garron, of course, and that ferret-faced fellow with the map,' the Doctor explained. 'They obviously planted the Jethryk in the Relic Cabinet.'

'Fascinating,' Romana murmured with heavy sarcasm.

'Indeed,' the Doctor nodded. 'They are trying to sell a fake map showing the position of a non-existent Jethryk mine.'

Romana leaped to her feet. 'That is no concern of ours,' she shouted. 'We have no time to meddle in local petty crime.'

Another ear-splitting snarl shook the tower.

'Please don't shout,' the Doctor winced. 'I have a headache.'

'All right: how did they get past that ... that thing down there?' Romana demanded with a shudder, stamping her feet against the cold.

'They doped it,' the Doctor replied simply, replacing the trap and locking the four tabs. 'I really ought to thank them for saving our lives ...'

Back in his own moth-eaten furs again, Unstoffe crunched through the snow-clogged alleyways near the outskirts of the city carrying a huge bundle. Making sure he was alone, he approached a large covered cart and carefully pulled aside the tattered awning. There spreadeagled among a pile of rags, lay the enormous semi-naked body of the young Shrieve, snoring loudly in deeply drugged sleep. Quickly Unstoffe opened the bundle and spread the Guard's uniform over him. As he did so, the Shrieve stirred: Unstoffe glimpsed his massively bulging muscles. At the same instant he was grabbed roughly from behind, dragged off the cart and carried bodily into a neighbouring alleyway where he was flung into a snowdrift.

'All right, my fancy young friend—what was all that about then?' growled a familiar voice.

Unstoffe twisted round and lay there, clawing the snow out of his eyes and trembling like a leaf.

The bulky figure of Garron was towering over him, his face purple with fury and his clenched hands raised threateningly. 'Skrynge stone ... lost mines ... dead prospectors ... phoney maps ... What are you trying to do—blow the whole scheme?' he hissed, reaching down and yanking Unstoffe up by the collar. 'I should break your miserable little neck, my lad.'

Unstoffe wriggled free. 'Listen, you old fool, I was just using my loaf ...' he protested, 'a bit of initiative: we could sell the map as an extra.'

Garron bore down on his cowering accomplice. 'Listen, boy, this is strictly a hit and run game—one bite and away—no banquets,' he said grimly. 'How often have I dinned it into your cloth ears: don't get greedy and don't give them time to think.'

Unstoffe bit his lip and looked sullen. Suddenly he flashed an impish smile. 'What did you think of the accent?' he chuckled.

Garron looked appalled. 'I'm the linguist in this outfit,' he snapped. 'I was sweating blood standing there while you did your party piece dressed like some prehistoric clown. I thought this Graff is no softy. He's a big bad soldier and if he tumbles that he's being conned . . .' Garron passed a stubby finger slowly across his throat.

Unstoffe shivered and glanced around. 'You're right, boss,' he murmured.

Garron pulled his fur hood tighter against the wind. 'Listen, Sholakh's fetching the deposit,' he said. 'A million.'

Unstoffe's beady eyes nearly popped out of his foxy little face. 'A mil . . . a million?' he gasped.

'So stick to the plan from now on—or else,' Garron warned. 'We'll meet by the shaft in an hour.'

Unstoffe shuddered. 'Go down there again . . . dope that beast again . . .' he whined. 'You don't know what it's like.'

Garron waved goodbye and turned to go. 'Just keep your mind on one million gold opeks and it'll be a doddle,' he retorted.

Suddenly Unstoffe's face lit up. 'That big, curly-headed bloke with the girl . . .' he called.

'I've got my eye on them, don't worry,' Garron flung over his shoulder as he waddled away.

'Maybe I could sell *them* the map,' Unstoffe chuckled to himself watching Garron disappear in the direction of the Citadel.

Just then there was a bellow of rage and the sound of splintering wood from the adjacent alley as the young Shrieve woke up. Unstoffe's cheeky grin vanished at once, and he fled away from the commotion as fast as he could scurry through the snowdrifts, making for the Citadel by a roundabout route as arranged.

The Graff Vynda Ka stared intently at the small circle of red-hot ash he had made on the edge of the flagstone hearth. Inside the glowing ring, facing each other on opposite sides, two scorpion-like creatures quivered with pincered stings raised for the attack. Impatiently the Graff prodded one with his thick gauntlet. The creature thrust its pincer into the glove several times

59

and then was still again. The Graff goaded the other. Nothing happened. He tried again. And again. But the creatures refused to attack each other. With a sigh of disappointment, the grim-faced young Prince shovelled the hot ash over them and then ground them with the heel of his boot.

Seconds later Sholakh entered, returning from the Levithian spacecraft with the million gold opeks concealed in his armour. Signalling to his Commander to keep silent, the Graff showed him the bugging device which he had replaced in its blackened niche inside the chimney. Then, without speaking, they hurried from the chamber.

'It is not a product of this planet, Highness,' Sholakh frowned as soon as they were outside.

'Garron planted it,' the Graff Vynda Ka snapped, his face an impassive mask. 'He must know everything.'

Sholakh smashed a gauntleted fist against the wall. 'I have suspected that bloated hog from the start,' he growled.

The Graff stalked off down the passage in the direction of the Relic Chamber. 'That Shrieve Guard whose father discovered the Jethryk ... a remarkable coincidence,' he murmured.

'Too remarkable, Highness,' Sholakh agreed. 'They must be working together.'

'However, Sholakh, that Jethryk nugget is large enough to make a man wealthy beyond his wildest dreams ...'

'Sufficient to power an entire fleet for several campaigns, Highness,' Sholakh added, turning to his master with shining eyes.

'Therefore they cannot be aware of its true value ...' the Graff concluded as they approached the top of the flight of steps leading down to the Relic Chamber. 'Keep a close watch on Garron, Sholakh. If he is playing games with the Graff Vynda Ka he will bitterly regret his folly.'

Sholakh nodded, smiling and rubbing his armoured hands together in anticipation. As they started to descend the steps the curfew gong began to sound, filling the Citadel with its warning clamour and sending the citizens hurrying homeward under the bleak twilight of Ribos.

The Captain of the Shrievalty paced impatiently around the Relic Chamber listening to the throbbing vibrations of the gong in the Citadel Tower above. All except one of the globes had been extinguished and the Shrieves were waiting to secure the chamber for the night. He was just about to give the order, when Garron burst through the doorway bathed in sweat, his whole body heaving breathlessly.

'Good ... good timing ...' he gasped.

'Where is the money?' the Captain demanded in a low voice, not without a trace of suspicion.

Garron looked round in dismay. 'My colleagues should be ... be here any moment ... I do assure you, Captain,' he panted, forcing a smile.

The Captain rattled his keys and stared at Garron's flustered, perspiring face. 'This is totally irregular ...' he murmured, glancing at his waiting Shrieves as the gong boomed relentlessly from the tower.

At last the Graff Vynda Ka stalked into the chamber accompanied by Sholakh.

Garron swept up to them. 'Greetings most esteemed sirs,' he cried, adding in an undertone, 'remember, Highness—you are merchants from the North.'

The Graff nodded with undisguised disdain.

'The money?' the Captain rapped out urgently.

Sholakh handed him a large sealed purse, and the Captain hurried across the chamber to one of the pillars supporting the vaulted roof. Selecting an elaborately patterned key from his ring, the Captain inserted it into a cleverly concealed lock and swung open one of the stone blocks like a door. He stuffed the

61

bulging purse into the hollow section and slammed the block shut. As soon as the lock had grated home, Garron waddled over and thrust a document and a stylo into the Captain's hand.

'If you would be so kind,' he beamed, 'just a signature on this receipt.'

The Captain hesitated, looking warily at the Graff Vynda Ka. Suddenly the Curfew gong went silent. Hastily the Captain scanned the paper.

'Let me hold these for you ...' Garron murmured, taking the keys while the Captain painstakingly scrawled his name on the document. Unseen by anyone, Garron deftly slipped one of the keys into the folds of his furs.

Taking back his key-ring, the Captain gave Garron the receipt and marched away to supervise the nightly ceremony. 'Prepare to release the Shrivenzale,' he ordered.

Garron paled visibly. 'A fascinating ritual, Highness, but one which we are not privileged to witness,' he beamed. 'We must return at once to our quarters.' He gave the Graff the receipt with a flourish.

The Graff Vynda Ka and Sholakh turned on their heels and strode away. Thanking the Captain profusely, Garron bowed low to the Relic Cabinet and scuttled out. He was late for another vital appointment...

'Hypothermia can kill,' Romana complained through chattering teeth, winding the Doctor's enormous scarf tighter round her neck and shoulders.

'So can loose talk,' the Doctor hissed, clapping his hand over his assistant's mouth as a small figure darted from the shadows and dumped a large bag at the edge of the trap.

They crouched in the lee of the parapet and watched closely as Unstoffe struggled to move the iron plate.

'It's our canny little friend with the treasure map ...' the Doctor breathed.

Just then a much bulkier figure lumbered across the rooftop and joined Unstoffe. 'What kept you?' he demanded suspiciously.

'Business,' Garron snarled, helping his feebler companion to open the trap.

At once a great roar and a cloud of warm, stale breath burst into the freezing air over the shaft. The two figures clutched one another in momentary panic. Then Unstoffe tipped the drugged meat into the shaft and reluctantly dragged the rope ladder from the sack.

'Stay here and keep watch,' the Doctor whispered, slowly rising to his feet and throwing a leg over the parapet.

'Where are you going *now*?' Romana asked, not at all happy at the prospect of being left alone on the tower with two criminals.

'I need to pop into the Relic Chamber before our friends get there,' the Doctor whispered, swinging himself silently over the stone coping.

'But Doctor ... that creature down there ...' Romana protested agitatedly, grabbing at his sleeve.

'Laurel and Hardy have just taken care of that for me,' he grinned. 'Before your time, my dear ...' he added in response to Romana's blank expression, and dropped abruptly out of sight.

'What if he's missed it?' Unstoffe objected, dubiously eyeing the key which Garron had just pressed into his clammy little hand.

'My boy, I was palming keys before you were even born,' Garron chuckled encouragingly. 'Anyway, he's got a dozen like that one.'

'In that case, it better be the right one,' Unstoffe retorted, ''cos I'm the mug who has to go down there.'

Garron squeezed his thin arm and beamed. 'And very proud of you I am, too,' he said. 'Now you'd better get going.'

At that moment another monstrous growl split the air. Unstoffe hesitated. 'Give it another five minutes ...' he pleaded. 'You haven't seen those teeth.'

Romana crouched in the darkening shadows, fuming at her inability to fathom the Doctor's eccentric and unpredictable behaviour, and at her failure to keep his attention focused on their important assignment. As she watched the activities of the two figures by the trap, she took out the Locatormutor Core and gripped it tightly with both hands, steeling herself to use the sensitive instrument as a bludgeon, should the need arise.

The Doctor waited until the Shrieve picket had marched away, and then darted down the worn steps to the lobby outside the Relic Chamber. Cautiously he approached the huge doors, noting as he passed that the shutter winch was in the 'open' position.

'Stay where you are,' rang a powerful voice.

The massive young Shrieve sentry was barring his way.

'Oh ... not asleep yet?' the Doctor asked sympathetically. 'Well, I couldn't sleep either,' he grinned, immediately discarding any idea of tackling the towering figure confronting him.

'You are under arrest. The Curfew has sounded,' the Shrieve announced, his huge hands gripping the sturdy pike shaft as if they were about to snap it like a twig.

'Yes, I heard it. It gave me quite a headache,' the Doctor frowned, racking his brain for a speedy tactical move. He knew that he had only a minute or two before Unstoffe reached the chamber.

'Where are you from?' the young giant demanded.

'The North,' the Doctor smiled, 'The South ...' he went on in desperation as the Shrieve took out a crude whistle from his belt and put it to his lips.

'Oh please don't wake everybody up on my account,'

the Doctor said earnestly, rummaging in his pockets and holding up the little dog whistle by its silver chain. 'This model is so much more effective ...' he murmured, swinging it rhythmically to and fro. 'So much quieter ... much quieter ... so quiet ...' His sonorous voice rose and fell in time with the oscillations of the tiny whistle.

The young Shrieve tried to tighten his grip on the pike as he fought off the instant drowsiness, his eyes sweeping from side to side and flickering at each swing of the glittering object in front of them.

'You must be so very sleepy ...' the Doctor suggested gently.

All at once the pike clattered onto the flagstones. The swaying Shrieve immediately jerked his drooping head upright again: 'I've been sleep ... ing all day ...' he murmured. 'Why should ... I want ... to sleep ... now?' And he lurched forward, his huge arms poised to envelop the Doctor and crush him to pulp.

His slight frame quaking with apprehension, Unstoffe edged past the colossal bulk of the Shrivenzale slumped on the floor of the antechamber and ducked under the raised shutter. Crossing to the Relic Cabinet, he quickly secured the suction cup to the front panel and then dissolved the colourless gum he had earlier used to reseal the panel with acid from a small bulb. After waiting a few seconds he lifted the heavy panel out of the frame. Then he reached and took the Jethryk nugget out of the case with sweating and trembling hands. Stuffing it into the pouch on his belt, he began to scurry round the dark eerie chamber, scanning the pillars for the hidden keyhole. The single globe above the cabinet gave so little light. Frantically he searched, frequently stopping to listen to the raucous breathing of the Shrivenzale in case the beast should stir.

At last he found the keyhole behind the pillar. 'One million gold opeks ...' he breathed as he unlocked and opened the stone block and grabbed the sealed purse from the niche.

At that moment something clattered heavily against the chamber doors outside. Instantly Unstoffe crammed the purse into his pouch and flattened himself against the pillar ...

Staring into the Shrieve's glazed eyes, the Doctor slowly backed away from the lumbering youth, still swinging the silver whistle on its chain. Suddenly the huge arms closed round him in a suffocating bearhug and he was swept off his feet like a dummy. But just as suddenly the Shrieve's prodigious grip loosened. He slid to his knees and pitched forward full length at the Doctor's feet.

Hugging his bruised ribs, the Doctor ran to the doors and within seconds had opened the massive locks with his tweezers and burst into the Relic Chamber. At once he saw that the cabinet had been broken into and that the Jethryk was missing.

'Too late ...' he muttered angrily, darting across to peer into the black rectangle of space beneath the shutter.

Something flew past his back. Even as he turned he heard the huge doors slam shut and the bar lock into place on the other side. Furious with himself, the Doctor hammered helplessly on the thick wooden doors. Then he heard the piercing blasts of a whistle from the lobby outside. At the same instant, a stentorian bellowing and shrill scrabbling sound burst from the antechamber beyond the shutter.

In three enormous strides the Doctor crossed the Relic Chamber and flung himself under the shutter. Frantically he reached out in the pitch darkness to find the end of the rope ladder which he guessed must surely be there. As he searched with blindly groping hands, he found himself suddenly showered with sparks as the Shrivenzale's flashing claws slashed through the blackness towards him ...

Garron peered anxiously into the shaft as the Shrivenzale's enraged roars and the crash of its tail grew more and more savage.

'Pipped at the post ...' he muttered in despair, wringing his hands and clutching his head. 'What a scheme ... a wasted talent ...'

Something stirring in the darkness made him pause. The rope ladder was swaying and creaking. Garron screwed up his eyes to see what was happening and a figure climbed rapidly into view.

'Unstoffe ... what went wrong?' he cried.

'Pretty well everything ...' boomed an unexpected voice, and the Doctor's head popped up suddenly in the trap opening.

Instantly recovering from the shock, Garron went to release the clips securing the ladder to the grappling hook.

'Don't move—we have you covered,' the Doctor cried.

'Who has?' Garron laughed scornfully.

'We have,' Romana declared, striding across the roof-top, brandishing the Locatormutor Core like a shillelagh as the Doctor climbed up out of the shaft.

Garron smacked himself on the forehead. 'I just don't believe it ...' he muttered, staring uncertainly at the strange weapon in Romana's hands. 'Alliance Security Agents. Well I'll be ...'

Slowly Garron got to his feet, shaking his head sadly. 'It's all right,' he murmured at last, 'I'll come quietly. It's a fair cop ...'

In complete silence the Doctor and Romana marched Garron at a cracking pace through the deserted alleyways on the outskirts of the city. As they entered the winding lanes leading towards the arched gateway, their prisoner grew more and more apprehensive. At last he could contain himself no longer.

'Where are you taking me?' he asked, in a

faint falsetto voice quite unlike his customary confident tone.

'To the TARDIS,' the Doctor replied. 'There are one or two loose ends to be tied up.'

'The ... the TARDIS?' Garron echoed, with frightened glances at his two escorts. 'What ... what happens there?'

'All kinds of things,' the Doctor said sternly. 'For example ...'

Before he could continue a dozen heavily armed Levithian Guards emerged from the snowdrifts ahead and blocked their path.

'For example ...' the Doctor repeated, trailing into silence as he slowed to a halt. He stood staring wide-eyed at the line of laser-spears, his hands sunk deep into his pockets and his feet shuffling the snow idly.

'We were expecting you, Garron, you and your accomplices,' rapped the Graff Vynda Ka's harsh voice behind them. They turned. The Graff and Sholakh were standing in the middle of the street flanked by more Guards whose black metallic armour gleamed stark and sinister against the snow.

They were trapped.

The Graff crunched towards them, his hard face unusually flushed and his cheek twitching uncontrollably. 'No one plays games with me. No one,' he said hoarsely, slapping one armoured hand with the gauntlet gripped in the other as he walked slowly round his victims.

The Doctor gestured calmly towards the bristling laser-spears levelled at them. 'I think there is some mistake ...' he said gently.

'There is no mistake!' the Graff screamed at him with blazing eyes. He turned on his heel and stamped back to where Sholakh was standing impassively waiting. 'Execute them,' he ordered.

The air was filled with a high-pitched whining as the Guards charged their spears. Garron flung himself face down in the snow. 'Mercy ... mercy ...' he whimpered.

Sholakh urgently murmured something to the Graff.

The Prince hesitated, then nodded: 'I agree, Sholakh,' he said striding forward again and yanking Garron to his knees by the hair. 'Get up you cringing cur,' he snarled, slashing Garron viciously across the face with his gauntlet.

Garron cowered at the Prince's feet, trying to cover his head with his arms, and whimpering pitifully.

The Graff raised his hand to strike again, but the Doctor strode forward and caught his arm. 'Not a very royal gesture your Highness ...' he cried. 'Assuming, of course, that you *are* a Highness.'

Wrenching his arm free, the Graff Vynda Ka stared at the Doctor speechless with disbelief. His hard mouth opened and shut but no sound came out. Slowly he backed away pointing a rigid arm at the Doctor. When he reached Sholakh, he began to utter incoherent guttural snarls between hysterical snatches of breath which shook his whole body. 'Kill ... kill him ...' he suddenly shrieked.

Once again Sholakh spoke rapidly to his master in a low earnest voice.

'Good advice, my faithful Sholakh,' the Graff muttered, growing a little calmer. 'We shall extract the whole truth from them, gradually and no doubt painfully, at our leisure.' With that he turned and stalked away towards the Citadel, closely followed by half a dozen of his bodyguards.

Sholakh turned to his prisoners with impatient delight. 'Take them,' he ordered. The remaining Guards closed in around the Doctor, Romana and Garron and prodded them into motion with their lethal spears.

Chapter 6

Unlikely Allies

The brooding silence of the Curfew over the city of Shurr was broken by the shriek of whistles and the thunder of hide boots as the Shrieve garrison rallied to the alarm raised by the sentry. The shutter was immediately lowered, confining the Shrivenzale in its den, while Shrieves armed with pikes and short swords searched the Relic Chamber and the Citadel.

Ashen-faced, the Captain of the Shrievalty examined the glass panel cut out of the Relic Cabinet. Moments earlier, he had discovered the theft of the million gold opeks from the cache in the nearby pillar. 'Nothing is missing from the Sacred Reliquary—the thief was obviously disturbed,' he murmured with intense relief. 'Even so he must be taken at once.' At his bidding, several Guards rushed from the chamber to join the search.

At that moment the Graff Vynda Ka entered, almost colliding with the burly Shrieves. 'What is happening?' he demanded.

The Captain explained. 'Such an act of sacrilegious vandalism shall not go unpunished,' he warned.

'Indeed, Captain,' the Graff nodded impatiently. 'But what of the one million opeks that I placed in your charge?'

The Captain glanced across at the pillar. 'Your gold has been taken sir,' he said quietly.

'Then you will recover it ...' the young Prince ordered in a hushed menacing voice. 'Otherwise, my Guards ...' The threat died on his lips and he shoved past the frowning Captain, his eyes darting among the sacred objects in the Relic Cabinet.

'Where is it?' he hissed, pointing to a small vacant area among the glittering treasures.

The Captain stared blankly into the cabinet. The Graff began crushing and twisting the bunched gauntlets in his hands. 'The Jethryk ... it has gone ...' he cried.

'Nothing is missing from the chamber except your gold, sir,' the Captain said firmly.

'The blue stone ... the Skrynge Stone ... look it was there ... just there ...' the trembling Prince gasped.

'Skrynge Stone?' the Captain said quietly, shaking his head and staring at the stranger as if he were a madman.

The Graff Vynda Ka suddenly became very still and calm, and a frozen smile set his face like a mask. 'Then it was a trick, just as I suspected ...' he said under his breath.

The Captain watched the silent stranger for a moment, trying to fathom his extraordinary behaviour. 'I have summoned the Seeker, sir,' he ventured.

'Seeker?' the Graff muttered, preoccupied with the deception Garron had tried to pull off at his expense.

'An ancient visionary, sir,' the Captain explained. 'No wrong-doer can escape the Seeker's eye. Rest assured, sir, the thief will be taken before daybreak.'

In the Graff Vynda Ka's quarters the Doctor, Romana and Garron stood with their backs up against the blazing fire in the centre of the chamber. They were completely surrounded by Levithian Guards whose expressionless slitted helmets and armour-plated bodies formed an impregnable wall around the helpless trio while they were searched. Sholakh had been methodically emptying the Doctor's many cluttered pockets, and the table was crowded with an assortment of strange objects—an ear trumpet, a corkscrew, string, marbles, a magnifying glass, a paper bag with a few jelly babies melted into a lump ...

Suddenly one of the Guards held up the Locator-mutor Core which Romana had vainly tried to conceal in her robe. Sholakh handled the unfamiliar device cautiously. 'What is this?' he demanded.

Romana glanced at the Doctor and shrugged in resignation: 'It's an instrument which ...'

'Does all kinds of tricks,' the Doctor butted in with a stern look at his frightened assistant. 'Like producing rabbits out of hats ... tracing underground streams ...'

'Let the female answer,' Sholakh snapped.

'You can even play a hornpipe on it,' the Doctor went on good-humouredly. 'Would you like me to show you?' He was viciously prodded back into place by a Guard.

'Do not bluff,' Sholakh retorted contemptuously. 'It is quite obviously some kind of weapon.'

The Doctor shrugged and stared at his feet in embarrassment like a scolded child. 'I can see you are no fool,' he mumbled, 'you are obviously an expert in weaponry.'

Sholakh allowed himself a faint smile of triumph as he stuck the Locatormutor Core into his belt.

'But mind it doesn't go off!' the Doctor suddenly cried covering his ears, 'I do so hate loud bangs.'

Sholakh laughed in the Doctor's face. 'Enjoy your childish fun while you can,' he sneered. 'The Graff Vynda Ka will soon wring the truth from you ... all of you.'

At that moment a loud warbling suddenly burst from Garron's sleeve. Panic-stricken, he flung his hands behind him desperately trying to wrench the radio from his wrist and drop it unnoticed into the fire. The brief signal ceased and there was silence. Garron stared innocently round at the others and gave an exaggerated shrug. Immediately the shrill warbling began again. Garron smashed his arm brutally against the edge of the chimney opening and the noise stopped abruptly.

Sholakh strode forward and ripped back the fur cuff of Garron's sleeve. As he pushed past, the Doctor slipped the Locatormutor out of Sholakh's belt with lightning fingers and thrust it up the arm of his overcoat.

'Of course ...' Sholakh smiled grimly, looking down at the crumpled mass of metal and twisted wire clamped to Garron's trembling wrist. 'More childish games.' He motioned the Guards out of the chamber and clattered after them, snatching up his massive helmet from the table.

'Your accomplice will not escape,' he flung at the silent trio from the doorway. 'When he is caught you will all perish—together.' With that, Sholakh put on his helmet and stared at them for a few seconds, his cruel laughter horribly muffled behind the angular metal mask.

The moment Sholakh left the chamber, the Doctor seized his ear trumpet from the cluttered table and leaped across to listen at the door.

Romana led the almost fainting Garron to a bench, sat him gently down and began delicately picking the slivers of metal and plastic out of his lacerated wrist.

'You're too kind, my dear,' he muttered, wincing and gritting his teeth. 'I never could stand the sight of blood—especially my own.'

The Doctor padded quietly over and sat hunched at the table. 'We're safer in here than we'd be in Fort Knox ...' he murmured gloomily to himself, halfheartedly gathering up his possessions and stuffing them haphazardly into his coat.

Romana took a tiny vaporiser from her robe and sprayed Garron's cleaned wound with sealant. 'Your communicator would have been useful,' she sighed.

Garron shrugged. 'It can't be helped. Unstoffe might have given away his position,' he said.

'Unstoffe ... your nimble apprentice no doubt,' the Doctor remarked. 'Yes, I almost bumped into him in the Relic Chamber—he's very light on his feet.'

73

Garron suddenly let out a guffaw of wry amusement. 'How ironic this all is,' he giggled. 'You and your charming colleague had just made a most elegant and efficient arrest ... and all to no good. Now we shall all die together.'

'I have absolutely no intention of dying just at present,' the Doctor retorted. 'It's quite definitely the very last thing I'm going to do.'

Garron shook his head knowingly: 'You won't have any choice—the Graff is a cold-blooded maniac.'

'Then you were rather foolish to try and sell him a non-existent mine,' the Doctor grinned.

Garron shrugged and glanced at his injured wrist which had now stopped bleeding. 'Well, the least I can do is to tell the Graff that you were nothing to do with my little scheme,' he smiled. 'Though I doubt whether he ...' Garron trailed off into silence and stared open-mouthed from the Doctor to Romana and back again. 'You ... you aren't Alliance Security Agents at all!' he cried, his cheeks wobbling with indignation as he lurched to his feet. 'Just what *is* your game?'

Before Romana could reply, the Doctor leaped up. 'Escapology,' he cried. 'I'm going to send an SOS.' And taking the silver dog whistle from behind his ear, he blew a series of inaudible blasts—alternately long and short.

The door of the silent and darkened TARDIS creaked slowly open and with agitatedly whirring antennae and brightly glowing eyes K9 emerged. He paused on the threshold, busily fixing a bearing on the Doctor's urgent signals. After a great deal of buzzing and clicking in his internal circuitry, he suddenly fell silent.

'Your position is established, master,' he announced loudly to no one in particular after several seconds pause. Then, with occasional short blasts of his infra-red radiaprobe to clear a path through the rapidly hardening snow, he set off into the night.

Reaching the arched gateway he stopped briefly to check his bearings and then buzzed quietly into the city, constantly weaving and rerouting himself in order to dodge the Shrieve patrols which were scouring the dark narrow alleyways in search of the thief.

K9 trundled rapidly through the deserted passageways of the Citadel busily searching for his master. Eventually he reached the bottom of the long flight of steep steps leading from the Relic Chamber to the upper storeys. There he stopped: the steps were impassable. For a few minutes he was motionless while his circuits hummed and his antennae waved about as he computed an alternative route.

Just as he was about to move off along a narrow gallery at the side of the steps, there was a gasp of amazement from the shadows by the doors to the Relic Chamber. K9 spun round. The massive young Shrieve Guard was staring in wide-eyed terror at the whirring alien object, his pike raised but his arms seemingly paralysed.

'No defensive action is necessary,' K9 rasped. 'My current programme is not hostile.'

For a moment the Shrieve did not move. Then he suddenly lunged forward, the pike aimed between the robot's glowing eyes. There was a brief flash which stopped him in his tracks, and then he sank to his knees and toppled over—stunned.

K9 swung round and buzzed away along the gallery, his radiaprobe primed and at the ready. Every so often he stopped as his receptors picked up another urgent signal from the Doctor, and each time he set off again with increased speed chattering quietly away to himself . . .

In the colonnaded Concourse at the centre of the city, Unstoffe himself was darting through the shadows desperately trying to evade the Shrieves. The nugget of

Jethryk and the purse full of gold opeks hung heavily at his side as he ran, stopping now and then to whisper urgently into his wrist radio: 'Garron ... Come in, Garron ... Come in ...' But whenever he put the tiny device to his ear all he heard was the mush of static. Anxiously he would click the transmit/receive button but it made no difference.

'Whatever's wrong with the old fool?' he muttered, hurling himself into a huge stack of firewood piled round one of the columns as a loud burst of whistling suddenly sounded nearby. 'Surely he hasn't gone to sleep up there in this weather ...' He lay motionless listening to the echoing whistles as the Shrieve patrols signalled to one another, and to the shrieking wind which hurtled through the colonnade throwing up uncannily life-like swirls of snow in the shape of ghostly creatures rising out of the shadows.

He knew that the longer he stayed in the city, the greater was the danger of being trapped. He decided that his only hope was to make a dash for the city wall and try to reach the small shuttle-craft which Garron had hired and which lay a couple of kilometres out in the tundra.

Cautiously he emerged from the pile of splintered timber, the wind cutting through him like a knife. Immediately he heard a crunch of boots swiftly approaching.

'There ... by the stack ... there's someone moving ...' yelled a Shrieve.

Unstoffe fled along the straggling line of makeshift dwellings packed between the thick columns on one side of the square. As he crept in among the hovels he realised that the Shrieves were closing in from both directions along the colonnade.

Just as he was preparing himself to make a desperate break across the deserted open square, Unstoffe's arm was gripped by a bony talon and he was dragged sideways under a flap of animal skin into one of the cramped, evil-smelling hutches.

'You'll be safe here ... quite safe,' croaked a wheezing, reedy voice in his ear, and he was thrust into a pile of furs and skins heaped on the hard ground. Unstoffe lay hidden, scarcely breathing, with his face buried in the flea-bitten rags. With racing heart he listened to the vicious slapping of the pikes against the flapping walls of the hovels as the Shrieves roused the inhabitants to search out their quarry.

The frail hut shuddered as its side was ripped open and a huge Shrieve thrust his head into the gloomy interior: 'Show a light there ...' he bellowed.

'Wha ... what's the ... what's the fuss ...' Unstoffe heard the croaking voice reply, obviously feigning sleepiness. His unknown protector turned up the wick of the guttering horn oil lamp a fraction.

'There's a thief hiding somewhere in the Concourse,' the Shrieve growled, jabbing his pike around at random. Unstoffe tried not to flinch as the sharp point hissed into the furs centimetres from his face. 'The Relic Chamber's been broken into. You haven't seen anyone ...? the Guard demanded, peering hard at the wizened, yellow-skinned figure huddling in rags beside the smoking lamp. The shrivelled old man shrugged.

'Don't I know your ugly face?' the young Shrieve suddenly growled, grabbing the old man's wasted neck in his huge paw and yanking his head into the light.

'You may do. I was celebrated throughout Ribos once,' the wheezing voice replied.

'It's Binro—Binro the Heretic!' the Shrieve exclaimed with a sneering grin. 'So this is how you ended up.'

'Go back and guard your trinkets and your superstitions,' Binro retorted with remarkable fearlessness.

The hulking young Shrieve tightened his grip. 'This old neck will snap like a dry twig,' he muttered, 'so don't tempt me.'

With a final glance round the squalid hut and a few parting jabs into the pile of skins, the guard tossed

Binro aside and lumbered out into the freezing darkness to continue the search.

For a few moments Unstoffe lay rigid in the pile of stinking furs, the Shrieve's pike still stabbing all around him in his imagination. Miraculously he could feel no wounds on his body. Then the furs were gently pulled off him and the emaciated figure of Binro handed him a horn beaker filled with some kind of warm soup.

'I know what it is to have every man's hand against you, my friend,' the shrunken old man croaked, his lively eyes bright with wisdom and kindness.

Unstoffe gratefully seized the beaker and drank the watery but warming liquid. 'You risked your life ... for me,' he murmured in disbelief as soon as he had drained the soup.

The old man smiled. 'My life is nothing ... not any more,' he smiled. 'I am an outcast.' He took the empty beaker and refilled it from a crude jug suspended over the guttering lamp.

'They called you Binro the Heretic,' Unstoffe said in a curious whisper. 'What did you do?'

'I told them the truth,' Binro replied with a shrug, handing the brimming beaker to the shivering fugitive.

Unstoffe stared blankly at the old man while he drank.

Binro cast his eyes upwards. 'You have looked at the sky at night time and seen the little points of light?' he asked in a hushed thin voice. Unstoffe nodded. Binro leant forward so that his wrinkled face almost touched Unstoffe's: 'They are not ice crystals at all,' he breathed. Then he sat back to watch the effect of his words.

Unstoffe was tempted to say, 'So what?' but something about Binro's bright clear eyes stopped him and he remained silent.

'I believe that all those tiny specks of light are suns just like our own sun ...' Binro went on, gazing earnestly at Unstoffe. 'I believe that each has worlds of its own—just like our own world of Ribos.'

Unstoffe smiled. 'It is an interesting theory,' he whispered.

Binro studied him a moment. 'You are an open-minded man—you must be from the Upper Pole,' he declared. 'I tell you I have made measurements of those points of light, and I have proved that Ribos *moves*. It travels round the sun like this and so we have the Ice Time and the Sun Time in succession.' Binro described an ellipse in the air with his hands.

'And so no one believed you,' Unstoffe murmured.

Binro gave a quiet croaking chuckle. 'They cling to their fantasies about ice gods and sun gods warring for supremacy over Ribos,' he muttered. 'They ordered me to recant.'

'And did you?' Unstoffe asked in hushed tones.

Binro held up his scarred and crippled hands. 'In the end I did,' he sighed. 'Now I am nothing.'

Unstoffe put his hand gently on the old man's withered arm. 'One day—in the future—you will be something again,' he said. 'All that you say is true. There *are* other suns and other worlds ...'

'You ... you believe it, too?' Binro breathed, his eyes suddenly brimming with tears.

Unstoffe put both his hands on Binro's fleshless shoulders. 'I know it is true,' he said. 'I come from one of those other worlds. I promise you, Binro, one day your people will turn to each other and say, "Binro was right. He told the truth."'

The wizened old man squatted there in the half-light huddled in his rotting rags, rocking himself slowly to and fro and listening to the distant whistles and shouts of the Shrieves searching the area round the Citadel. Then he clasped Unstoffe by the hand. 'They will never find you while I live,' he pledged solemnly. 'Never.'

* * *

79

The walls of the Relic Chamber were a mass of grotesque shadows and flickering shapes. In the centre, just in front of the Reliquary, a small circle of iron-work braziers had been set up, each one containing a flaring bundle of tallow-soaked rags. In the midst of the smoking fires stood a scrawny hag dressed in long strips of crudely dyed remnants. Her frizzled grey hair was parted on the crown of her domed head, and it reached almost to her feet in a thickly tangled cascade. A semi-circle of Shrieves flanked their Captain, silently watching as the Seeker prepared herself for the ancient ritual of casting the bones. The Graff Vynda Ka and Sholakh lingered nearby in the shadows.

The Seeker raised her stick-like arms, flourishing the two cracked and splintered bones clasped in her knotted hands. Throwing back her head, she opened her toothless mouth wide and uttered a long incantation made up of croaks and snarls, shrieks and whinings which merged and echoed in the vaulted chamber. She clattered the two bones together above her head in a complex rhythmic tattoo, and then stretched out her arms sideways and began to spin round faster and faster . . .

'Primitive mumbo jumbo,' Sholakh scoffed under his breath.

The Graff leaned towards Sholakh without taking his eyes from the rapidly spinning figure in the circle. 'The Captain assures me that it never fails,' he murmured.

The Seeker stopped abruptly and began to chant in unexpectedly sonorous tones. 'Bones of our Fathers, bones of our Kings by the Spirit that once moved you, seek and find. Seek in the Ice Time. Seek in the Sun Time. Seek and find. Come into the Circle, Spirits of the Ice, Spirits of the Sun, show what I seek. Show . . . Show . . .'

Suddenly quite still, she let the bones clatter on to the flagstones. They came to rest exactly in line and as they did so the brazier to which they pointed flared up momentarily with a fierce roar. The Seeker stared into the flames until they had died down again.

'I see him ... I see him ...' she whispered. 'At the place of the fires.'

The Captain stepped forward. 'The Concourse,' he exclaimed. 'But we have searched there. We found nothing.'

The Seeker turned blazing eyes upon the Captain. 'Then seek again,' she muttered hoarsely. 'He is there ... I see him.' Stooping, she gathered up the bones. Then with a sudden hissing sound she whirled round once: all the fires were instantly extinguished.

Holding the bones at arm's length, the wizened hag slowly left the chamber, closely followed by the Captain and his Guards. As she shuffled along she repeated under her breath, over and over again: 'I see him ... I see him ... I see him ...' in a hypnotic refrain.

'It's just trickery,' Sholakh muttered, gazing at the ring of rapidly cooling braziers.

The Graff Vynda Ka shook his head. 'We shall follow. Fetch my faithful Levithians, Sholakh. If the thief is found we shall take the Jethryk and our gold. But be prepared: we may have to fight our way out of the city ...'

Romana paced agitatedly round and round the fire in the Graff's quarters while the Doctor and Garron sat at the table chatting together like two old cronies whiling away a long winter evening over a bottle of whisky. Occasionally the Doctor crept to the door, listened intently for a moment and then blew several blasts on the dog whistle.

'... but I had a spot of bother with a dissatisfied client and was forced to leave Earth to seek my fortune elsewhere.' Garron smiled, shaking his head over his reminiscences.

'What happened?' the Doctor enquired.

'He was an Arab, of course,' Garron went on, 'and

when I offered him Sydney Harbour Bridge for fifty million dollars he got greedy and insisted I throw in the Opera House as well. Well naturally I refused.'

'Naturally,' the Doctor smiled ironically.

'I could hardly let that priceless monument to our cultural heritage fall into his hands,' Garron protested with a shocked frown. 'Unfortunately the Arab took umbrage and showed all the impressive documents I'd cooked up to the Antartican Government—so I had to emigrate.'

The Doctor padded over to listen at the door. 'No doubt your victim came looking for you,' he murmured.

'With a posse of Bedouin touting neutron guns,' Garron nodded ruefully. 'I've never been back.'

The Doctor chuckled sympathetically.

Romana's exasperation boiled over. 'Doctor. How can you gossip with this petty confidence trickster when there are people out there intending to kill us?' she exploded.

'Don't you worry yourself about that, my dear,' the Doctor replied gently. 'I'm keeping an ear on them.'

He sat down again at the table and leant towards Garron. 'But what really intrigues me is how you first got your hands on that piece of Jethryk,' he murmured, gazing in flattering admiration.

Garron eyed the Doctor warily but could not help swelling with pride. 'I ... I acquired it,' he smiled evasively.

'You stole it,' Romana corrected him sharply.

Garron's fleshy lips curled with contempt. 'That is a very damaging remark,' he retorted, 'but only to be expected on a Class Three Planet such as this.'

The Doctor's eyebrows shot up. 'Class Three Planet?' he exclaimed. 'What do you mean?'

Garron drew himself up in the chair and beamed. 'Just a technical term, sir,' he said condescendingly, 'a convenient method of classifying properties.'

The Doctor stared wide-eyed. 'Properties?' he echoed.

'Indeed sir: I deal in planetary real estate,' Garron explained. 'I sell planets.'

The Doctor's jaw dropped a fraction of a centimetre.

'Of course at first I thought you were Alliance Security,' Garron continued. 'They've been on my tail ever since I sold Mirabilis Eighty-One to no less than three different purchasers ... That was my greatest deal,' he sighed nostalgically, before lapsing into silence.

'What about your latest customer—the Graff Vynda Ka—or whatever he calls himself. What does he want Ribos for?' the Doctor asked, going once more to the door and listening.

Garron outlined the Graff's ambitious scheme. 'It's a hopeless madman's dream,' he chuckled. 'but his gold is real enough.'

'He may be a madman but he certainly saw through *you*!' Romana snapped with scathing irony.

'Young Unstoffe's fault entirely, dear lady,' Garron replied. 'He went right over the top. He's a dreadful ham at heart, I'm afraid.'

The Doctor returned and sat by the table. 'And the Jethryk ... Just bait?' he suggested innocently.

Garron nodded. Then he looked very hard at the Doctor. 'You seem to be extremely interested in that nugget, sir. You haven't told me what *your* racket is yet,' he said slyly.

The Doctor threw his arms up in the air vaguely. As he did so the Locatormutor Core flew out of his sleeve and was instantly caught by Romana before it could crash into the fire.

'You could be extremely useful in the slips, my dear,' the Doctor said, turning to her with a broad smile. Then he answered Garron's question with a casual shrug: 'Oh we're just here on holiday, but we seem to keep getting caught up in things ...'

'Things which do not in the least concern us,' Romana snapped, examining the Locatormutor for any sign of damage.

'Indeed,' the Doctor agreed, jumping to his feet. 'We really ought to be moving on. However there doesn't appear to be a convenient window, the chimney is much too hot to climb and our Round Table friends outside sound rather ...'

The Doctor stopped in mid-sentence and listened to the muffled noise of activity suddenly penetrating through the sturdy wooden door. Pulling out his ear trumpet, he crept over and applied its tarnished horn to the gap running between the hinges. He listened as Sholakh briefed the Levithian Guards, telling them that the Shrieves planned to raid the Concourse again at dawn and that the Graff's forces would be expected to recover the Jethryk and the gold. 'We shall vanish before they realise what hit them,' he concluded. 'Rakol, Norka and Krolon will guard the prisoners until the operation is completed. At our signal, execute them.'

The Doctor crept away from the door and told the others what he had overheard.

'So we have until dawn,' Romana murmured.

'Which must be almost upon us,' the Doctor frowned. 'I do hope that K9 hasn't fallen asleep.'

Eventually Garron broke the gloomy silence which had descended on the three prisoners. 'If only we had some bargaining power!' he exclaimed, thumping the table. With a gasp of pain he thrust his injured hand under the other arm to ease the sudden throbbing. 'If I still had the radio I could warn the boy,' he winced. 'As long as he stays free we have something to negotiate with ...'

The Doctor rummaged through the remains of the tiny device scattered on the table. 'I'm afraid you made far too good a job of it,' he sighed.

Suddenly Garron jumped up, the pain seemingly

gone. He hurried to the chimney, felt about and held up the bugging receiver. 'A little something I rigged up to keep an eye on my customer,' he explained.

In one bound the Doctor crossed the chamber and snatched the device from Garron's plump fingers. 'All we need now is a call-up circuit so that we can attract Unstoffe's attention,' he muttered excitedly. He took out his magnifier and studied the bug carefully, then he sat down at the table and started sorting through the fragments from Garron's radio set.

'Search the floor ... search in every crack and bring me any pieces you can find—however small,' the Doctor instructed. Then with nimble fingers he began to dismantle the bugging receiver. 'I assume that Unstoffe's two-way is on the same wavelength as this gadget?' he suddenly asked.

Garron nodded. He and Romana knelt down and eagerly started searching the chamber floor for the vital components.

They soon managed to salvage quite a few usable pieces from the shattered wrist set and they watched anxiously as the Doctor worked feverishly to adapt the bugging device into a transmitter.

'Of course I can't promise that this little lash-up will work,' the Doctor murmured, trying to twist several tiny platinum wires together with his large fingers. 'However, since we have no receiver we shan't know whether Unstoffe can hear us or not.'

'It must be dawn by now,' Romana breathed. Garron nodded grimly and gave her a faintly sympathetic smile.

'Put your little finger just there, my dear,' the Doctor muttered, indicating a complex knot of wires with his tweezers. Romana obliged while the Doctor made the final connections.

'Now, keep your fingers crossed—not you, Romana,' he frowned, bridging two sets of contacts with the tweezers for several seconds. 'There. That should have caught his attention,' the Doctor said, removing the tweezers. 'You'd better talk to him Garron—he knows your voice.'

'But does he trust you?' Romana said under her breath, taking her finger from the bristling connection.

Garron bent over the table and spoke into the curious apparatus which the Doctor had put together: 'Hello ... Hello Unstoffe ... This is Garron ...'

Just then there was a sudden commotion outside the chamber: the clatter of heavy armour and urgent muffled shouting.

'It's too late,' Romana cried. 'It's too late—they've come to kill us all.'

Motioning Garron to keep talking the Doctor rushed over and listened at the door. In just a few seconds they would know their fate.

Chapter 7

Escape Into the Unknown

Outside the chamber the three Levithian sentries had
been startled by the sudden appearance of K9 round a
corner some way along the passage. With swift dis-
ciplined movements they formed a compact defensive
group, charged their laser-spears and took careful aim
at the strange device bearing down on them. Meanwhile K9's circuits were buzzing away, rapidly com-
puting their average bodyweight and the thickness of
their armour plating in order to calculate a suitable
stun level.

Microseconds before the Levithians could press their
discharge buttons they were all three silhouetted in a
brilliant flash from K9's muzzle, which sent them reel-
ing back against the door to their Prince's quarters.
Like three monstrous puppets they slid clumsily down
the rough woodwork into a tangled heap on the flagstones.

K9 came to rest in front of them. 'Most satisfactory,'
he announced.

The Doctor flung open the door, revealing the three
Levithian Guards spreadeagled on the threshold and
K9 standing impassively over his victims buzzing
quietly to himself.

'What kept you K9?' the Doctor cried delightedly,
stepping over the unconscious sentries. 'We've been on
tenterhooks for hours.'

'Topographical difficulties, master,' K9 replied.

The Doctor patted the creature's whirring head:
'Of course—you can't manage stairs, poor old thing,'
he murmured kindly.

Romana clambered past the huddled bodies followed closely by Garron. 'Are they dead?' she asked with a grimace of distaste.

The Doctor gave her a shocked look. 'Of course they aren't dead,' he cried. 'What an idea.'

'Negative, Mistress,' K9 added. 'Stun was calibrated at zero nine atmospheres.'

'They'll be out for hours,' the Doctor muttered, dragging the first of the limp bodies through into the Graff's quarters.

'Correction, master: period of immobilisation estimated at three point two nine hours,' K9 announced crisply.

'All right, all right. Stop showing off,' the Doctor scolded irritably as he and Garron dealt with the other two Guards.

Shutting the door firmly behind him, the Doctor asked Garron to lead the way to the Concourse. Sticking the laser-spear and charger unit which he had taken from Krolon into his belt, Garron set off quickly along the passage.

'Don't stop at every corner, K9,' the Doctor called. 'We have very little time.'

Romana looked extremely unhappy as she and the Doctor hurried along behind the waddling con-man. 'You are going to trust that petty trickster, Doctor?' she whispered incredulously.

The Doctor nodded vigorously: 'No more than he is going to trust us, my dear . . .' he murmured.

'Then why are we helping him?' Romana demanded in an undertone grabbing the Doctor's sleeve and attempting to slow him down.

The Doctor continued to forge ahead. 'We are not helping him,' he muttered out of the corner of his mouth. 'He is helping *us*.'

Romana cast her eyes upward and shook her head, dumb with exasperation. She had the Locatormutor Core safely tucked into her robe, and it was becoming increasingly apparent to her that she would be forced

88

to continue the search for the First Segment of the Key to Time all by herself ...

The strident warbling from Unstoffe's wrist seemed to shatter the silence around Binro's tiny hovel and echo among the columns of the colonnade. Unstoffe immediately flung his arm into the furs and pulled a bundle of rotting skins over them to help deaden the sound. Binro squatted wide-eyed and open-mouthed, staring at Unstoffe until—after what seemed like an age—the warbling stopped.

At once Unstoffe put the wrist set to his ear. Garron's rapid, clipped voice burst through loudly and clearly: 'This is Garron ... repeat, this is Garron ... Listen carefully—you can't call me back any more so don't waste time trying—you've been traced to the Concourse and the Shrieves will be making a full-scale raid any minute ... Get out now ... I repeat ...'

Unstoffe snapped off the speaker. 'We heard you the first time, Daddyo,' he muttered.

Binro looked warily at the device strapped to Unstoffe's wrist. 'Truly you are from another world,' he marvelled.

'I need to be on the move again,' Unstoffe said scrambling to his feet, 'but where can I go now so they won't find me?'

Binro sprang up with surprising agility, thrusting a tattered skin into Unstoffe's trembling hands. 'Cover yourself with this, my friend,' he croaked. 'You have only one chance now—you will have to take refuge in the Catacombs.'

Unstoffe hesitated, his mouth suddenly feeling very dry and his heart beginning to race. 'The Catacombs?' he gasped, shivering and swallowing hard. 'What are they?'

'Come,' Binro murmured, blowing out the oil lamp and thrusting it into his rags. 'You must follow me.'

They slipped out of the flapping hovel and into the wind-swept colonnade just as the first green streaks of daylight began to slash across the sky.

Reaching the far side of the city, they descended a long steep incline which led into the ground, keeping themselves in the shadow of the stone embankment rising higher and higher on each side of them. The dull green and orange sky cast a poisonous aura over the snowdrifts, and Unstoffe constantly shivered with cold and apprehension. At the bottom of the cutting they reached a broad, low entrance whose arched portico was carved into fantastic gargoyles, their monstrous shapes exaggerated by a stark layer of hardened snow.

'Good. It is as I expected. The Shrieves have all gone to search the Concourse,' Binro muttered as they approached the deserted doorway. Striking a flint against the rough stonework, Binro coaxed a spluttering flame from his horn lamp.

The massive door creaked slowly open as they both put their shoulders to its gnarled frame. In the pitch darkness inside, Binro's lamp shed a faint eerie light onto damp moss-covered walls as warily they ventured into the oppressively stale gloom. Binro teased up the wick to give more light and led the way forward. With a tearing, echoing rasp the great doors began to close behind them. Instinctively Unstoffe turned back, but Binro held him tightly to the spot until it shut with a shattering thud.

'What ... what is this place?' Unstoffe stammered, glancing fearfully around him.

'We call this the Hall of the Dead,' Binro replied, his voice strangely muffled in the damp heavy air. 'And beyond this stretch the Catacombs themselves ...'

They had entered a colossal vault—excavated out of the swampy clay and lined with crudely fashioned stone blocks—which was criss-crossed by a maze of tall galleries, several stories high. Along each gallery were ranged tier upon tier of horizontal niches with rectangular openings in the gloom.

Unstoffe glanced into the nearest hole and shuddered. In it lay a filthy threadbare shroud with human bones sticking out from tears in the rotting fabric, like the blunt spines of some fantastic porcupine. As his eyes grew gradually accustomed to the dank murk, he realised that he was being 'watched' by endless rows of staring skulls lolling and grinning in their stone graves.

'There must be thousands and thousands of them ...' he marvelled as they made their way past junction after junction with the tiers of niches stretching away on both sides.

'Yes,' Binro croaked. 'Everyone comes here in the end.'

'Well I don't want to stay ... not just yet,' Unstoffe muttered faintly, keeping as close to his guide as possible.

Binro held the flickering lamp a little higher as they turned into one of the side galleries for what seemed to Unstoffe like the hundredth time.

'Courage, my friend, the Catacombs are just ahead of us,' he said quietly. 'You are not afraid are you?'

He led Unstoffe down a seemingly endless sloping tunnel with rough-hewn rocky walls and a treacherously uneven floor which connected the Hall of the Dead with the Catacombs beyond. Here and there the tunnel swelled into large caverns, and as it gradually penetrated deeper into the rock it branched into more and more similar tunnels leading off in all directions. Eventually they entered the labyrinth itself, struggling forward with only the feeble light from the horn lamp to guide them.

'How far do these Catacombs stretch?' Unstoffe asked in an awed whisper as he stumbled along behind his agile guide.

'No one knows,' croaked Binro. 'They are partly natural and partly excavated by our ancestors thousands of Ice Times ago to provide a temple for their Ice Gods.' He waited for Unstoffe to catch up.

91

'But ... but ... you don't believe in the ... Ice Gods?' Unstoffe stuttered, clinging to Binro's twiglike arm.

Binro gave a toothless grin. 'Of course not.'

A harsh roaring suddenly tore out of the pitch darkness ahead of them and echoed round the maze of tunnels and chambers for several seconds.

'What was that?' Unstoffe breathed, his thin face like chalk.

'A Shrivenzale. There is a colony of the creatures down here,' Binro replied calmly.

Unstoffe gulped and clung onto him for dear life. 'Like the thing that keeps watch in the Relic Chamber?' he said.

Binro nodded. 'But that is quite a small one.'

Another shattering snarl seemed to split the cavern asunder. This time it was much closer and it was followed by unmistakable panting and scratching sounds.

To Unstoffe's horror Binro began to creep cautiously onwards. 'Let's go back,' he pleaded, tugging nervously at Binro's arm.

Binro firmly kept going. 'If you go back you will surely be caught, my friend, and the fate of thieves is terrible in Shurr,' he murmured, gripping Unstoffe's arm persuasively.

'Nothing could be worse than ending up as that thing's breakfast,' Unstoffe protested, desperately trying to free himself.

Binro held onto him like a limpet. 'There must be a way up to the surface if only we can find it,' he urged. 'The Shrivenzales hunt for food in the tundra. They only come here to shelter and sleep.'

Unstoffe listened to the stirrings of the nearby monsters with sinking stomach as Binro dragged him deeper into the underground labyrinth. 'So you reckon we can just tiptoe past them, do you?' he said in a wavering voice as they entered a large cavern echoing with the creatures' drowsy snufflings.

'We do not have any choice, my friend,' Binro whis-

pered, and shielding the light from the lamp he began
to lead the way among a cluster of gigantic boulders
scattered over the floor of the cavern like slumbering
beasts ...

The Shrieves had surrounded the Concourse in the
steadily growing daylight, and in the middle of the
square the Seeker was swaying slowly from side to side
uttering a long, incomprehensible chant with the
bones pressed against her temples. The Captain of the
Shrievalty waited nearby, the fur of his helmet stream-
ing in the relentless icy wind. In the shadows under
the colonnade the Graff Vynda Ka and Sholakh were
watching impatiently.

Eventually the Seeker squatted on her haunches and
sank into a deep trance.

'Our forces have established concealed positions covering all exits, Highness. We are in control of the entire area,' Sholakh murmured. 'No one will escape.'

The Graff nodded, his face an expressionless mask
with hooded eyes and thinly compressed lips.

'No one,' he echoed, his thick gauntlets creaking as
he twisted them slowly in his pale, blue-veined hands.

As the Doctor, Romana and Garron approached the
Concourse, K9 suddenly halted them with a brisk
warning: 'Hostile presence ahead—nineteen point
five metres.'

The Doctor went cautiously to the corner of the
alleyway and immediately returned. 'The Graff's
Guard's are covering the entrance,' he whispered.

Garron said he knew another way into the square
round the back of the arcade and squeezed himself
along a narrow gully to reconnoitre.

As soon as he had gone, Romana steeled herself for
yet another skirmish with the Doctor while they waited
behind a thick buttress.

'The Relic Chamber is no doubt unguarded, Doctor,' she murmured, trying to sound as reasonable as possible. 'Therefore we should take advantage of this distraction to retrieve the Segment.' To her surprise the Doctor did not snap at her or scowl. Instead he grinned.

'But the Segment is not in the Relic Chamber,' he explained.

Romana looked stunned. 'But the Crown of Ribos is ...' she began, pulling the Locatormutor Core from her robe.

The Doctor took the Core and switched it on. 'Look,' he said tuning the signal, 'there, you see?'

Romana stared at the Core dumbfounded. 'But ... it's pointing to the other side of the city,' she exclaimed.

'Precisely my dear; it is pointing to our friend, Unstoffe; and more precisely still, to the lump of Jethryk he is carrying,' the Doctor smiled.

'The Jethryk? But I thought ...' Romana went suddenly quiet—inwardly furious at her lack of perception.

The Doctor switched off the Core. 'I'm surprised you didn't realise it yourself—bright girl like you,' he grinned. 'I did warn you about getting led up the garden path ...'

'But what made you realise it was the Jethryk?' Romana gasped admiringly.

After glancing warily about, the Doctor quickly explained: 'You remember we computed two different bearings on the location of the Segment in the TARDIS? Obviously the Segment was moved a considerable distance in between those two readings. Now the Crown of Ribos is never moved—never even touched—whereas the Jethryk was brought to Ribos by Garron shortly before we ourselves arrived. Simple really.'

Just then Garron came scrambling back along the gully. 'All clear this way,' he panted.

'Excellent,' the Doctor answered. 'By the way, your

friend Unstoffe got your message.'

How do you know that?' Garron exclaimed.

The Doctor flourished the Locatormutor. 'This little gadget tells us where the Jethryk is and its pointing way over there ...'

'Unstoffe has the Jethryk!' Garron said, with a sidelong look at the Doctor and then at the Core he was waving.

'Exactly. Follow me, gang,' the Doctor cried diving eagerly into the gully.

Garron hurried after him side by side with Romana, trying hard to conceal his eager fascination with the Locatormutor from the sharp eyes of the unfriendly young female. He did not know who these two strangers were, but he was determined to make good use of them if he could in order to get his hands on the precious nugget first ...

For some time the Graff Vynda Ka had been stamping about with cold and irritation under the arcade when at last the Seeker rose on her spindly legs, whirled around and cast her two bones onto the paving. Then she bent over them muttering to herself.

'He has gone,' she suddenly cried with a malicious grin at the watching Shrieves.

The Captain strode forward. 'Gone?' he shouted, glancing round the Concourse. 'Impossible. My Shrieves are positioned at all possible exits.'

The Seeker gathered up her bones and closed her eyes, shutting out all protests. 'He is no longer in this place. The one you seek is in the Catacombs,' she croaked hoarsely.

The Captain stood threateningly over the old crone but she sat back on her haunches shaking her frizzled head, her mouth agape in a toothless hole and her eyes narrowed into bright green slits.

Closely followed by Sholakh, the Graff marched over to the Captain. 'You assured me the thief would be taken,' he snarled kicking the squatting priestess. 'Get this rotting hag to sniff him out at once.'

The Captain shook his head. 'The thief has taken refuge in the Catacombs, sir. He will die there. The matter is ended,' he said calmly, turning to dismiss the search party.

The Graff's nostrils began to flare and his face to twitch violently. 'It is not ended,' he barked. 'He has my gold.'

The Captain met his challenging stare with unruffled firmness. 'My Shrieves will not go into the Catacombs after your gold,' he retorted.

'Why not? What are these Catacombs?' Sholakh demanded.

'An ancient labyrinth beneath the city,' answered the Captain. 'The home of the long-dead and of the Ice Gods. No one who has ventured beyond the Hall of the Dead has ever returned.'

'My Guards are made of sterner stuff,' Sholakh snorted, 'they are not afraid.'

The Captain looked hard at Sholakh. 'Your Guards?' he murmured. 'But you are men of business.'

At once the Graff stepped in with a placatory smile. 'Of course, Captain. They are members of a special unit recently formed in the Upper Provinces for the protection of the trading routes.'

'Then let them protect your gold, sir,' retorted the Captain, turning on his heel and walking brusquely away.

The Graff went after him. Barely able to contain his outraged anger, he struggled to remain calm. 'You can direct us to these ... these Catacombs, Captain?' he requested.

The Captain considered a moment. 'Life is more precious than gold,' he said quietly. Beside him the Seeker was rocking back and forth. Suddenly she uttered a dry cackle and catching the Captain's eye she nodded malevolently.

The Captain shrugged. 'Very well, if you are determined to go, sir,' he agreed reluctantly. 'But I warn you—none of you will ever return.'

The Seeker leapt to her feet and beckoned them to follow, gesticulating and chuckling to herself as she led the way eagerly out of the Concourse and away from the Citadel towards a remote and abandoned part of the city.

With K9 whirring along just ahead of them, the Doctor, Romana and Garron hurried down the icy slope towards the entrance to the Hall of the Dead. The Locatormutor Core was bleeping steadily in the Doctor's hands, indicating the whereabouts of Unstoffe and the nugget of Jethryk.

'He can't be very far ahead now,' the Doctor muttered as the signal became gradually faster and faster.

Cautiously they entered the vast necropolis, the massive door swinging shut behind them with shrieking hinges. As K9 lit the way between the rows of tiered galleries with his photon radiaprobe throwing up great fluttering shadows, the Doctor clambered nimbly about, shining his pocket torch into the gaping rectangular tombs.

'Fascinating ...' he murmered, surveying the crumbling skeletons and tattered shrouds of the long-dead occupants. 'Quite extraordinary.'

Romana shrank against Garron's perspiring bulk as several skulls suddenly clattered down from their resting places and rolled grotesquely about on the paving before coming to rest at her feet.

'Your young associate certainly has a good nose for hiding places,' the Doctor remarked to Garron as he swung himself back down to the ground and switched on the Locatormutor again.

The signals were distinctly weaker. 'Come along, we must catch up at once,' Romana said, stepping gingerly over the skulls and looking daggers in the Doctor's direction.

'Took the words right out of my mouth, my dear,' the Doctor cried, adjusting the signal and then setting off along a side-turning with K9 buzzing along beside him. Romana and Garron hurried to catch up.

Constantly changing direction at the endless junctions between the galleries, they followed the indications given by the monotonously bleeping Core deeper and deeper into the mausoleum. Garron scarcely took his eyes off the strangely glowing device carried by the Doctor, but from time to time he glanced furtively at his two companions as if he were hatching some crafty plot at the back of his devious mind.

Suddenly K9 stopped dead, antennae furiously revolving. 'Sentient life forms approaching,' he announced curtly.

'*Approaching?*' the Doctor queried, checking the Core signal.

'Affirmative, master,' K9 declared. 'Ninety metres ... from the rear.'

The Doctor spun round and shone his torch back along the gully they were following. 'Well, if you say so, K9,' he shrugged.

'Eighty-three metres and closing ...' the robot rapped out. 'Optimum counter-action immediate concealment in adjacent cavities.'

The Doctor glanced quickly round. 'I've had a much better idea,' he said, heaving K9 into the nearest ground-level tomb and motioning Romana and Garron into a neighbouring one. Then he clambered up into one of the niches above them and settled his large awkward frame down beside the shrouded skeleton as best he could.

They huddled in the airless, dusty recesses and lay utterly still, scarcely daring to breathe. They heard the heavy tramp of marching boots and the sinister clatter of armour advancing steadily through the Hall of the Dead towards them. The dark vault above was slashed by powerful torch-beams and echoed with urgent shouts.

Sholakh halted his Levithian Guards at the fallen skulls and ordered a thorough search of the surrounding galleries. But the Graff Vynda Ka swept on ahead. 'Do not waste time here,' he cried. 'The thief will have gone deeper than this.'

Shortly afterwards the Graff's search-party entered the section where the Doctor and the others were hidden, and surged along the gully, their torches prying irresistibly into every nook and cranny. As they drew rapidly closer the Doctor tried frantically to attract K9's attention, but without success. Easing himself to the edge of the stone pallet, he cautiously peered over and called his mechanical pet as loudly as he dared. Still there was no reaction from K9.

The Doctor ducked back just in time as the bristling torch beams played over the gallery. Unfortunately his shoulder nudged the rotten shroud beside him and it split open, releasing the gaping white skull to topple over the edge and smash into smithereens on the floor of the gully below him.

'We have him. Charge weapons,' Sholakh barked.

The Doctor froze in his cramped niche as the Guards primed their laser-spears with an echoing whine. Then during the unbearable silence which followed, he felt about in his overflowing pockets for the dog whistle. After a brief and desperate search he found it, but before he could manoeuvre the tiny object to his lips there was a vicious sizzling sound, and razor sharp fragments of stone began to fly in all directions as the laser-spears raked the rows of tombs with methodical efficiency from end to end.

While the jagged masonry sliced through the air around them, the Doctor and his companions suddenly made out another sound above the hiss and whine of the lasers: a series of harsh gurgling roars which shook the huge mausoleum like an earthquake. The bombardment ceased abruptly, and they heard Sholakh screaming orders to his Levithians as a colossal Shrivenzale appeared at the far end of the gully in the direction of the Catacombs.

The Guards stared in disbelief at the cascades of brilliant sparks spraying from the creature's scrabbling claws and serrated tail, lashing the splintered stonework. They took cover among the branching galleries, hurriedly priming their weapons as the Shrivenzale crawled angrily towards them. It tossed and reared in the bright torchlight roaring with pain as burst after deadly burst ripped into its thickly scaled body and its armoured hide began to melt and split. But still it dragged itself towards its attackers, sending them scrambling into fresh cover as it bore down on them.

Sholakh rallied his scattered forces in a side gallery and ordered a ceasefire. All the torches were switched off and the Levithians waited in silence.

Gradually the Shrivenzale's monstrous bellowing subsided. The Doctor lay motionless in his niche, listening to the laboured breathing of the wounded creature only a few metres away from him as it hesitated in the darkness, sniffing the air suspiciously. To his immense relief he heard the beast slowly dragging its massive bulk round, and the crumbling galleries shuddered as it began to retreat towards the Catacombs.

As the Shrivenzale lumbered back to its lair, the Graff Vynda Ka and Sholakh listened until its raucous gasping had died away. Then Sholakh snapped on his torch and swept it over the confusing prospect of identical junctions and tiers of graves.

'We must go on until we find him,' the Graff rapped, shining his own lamp directly into his Commander's frowning face. 'Well, Sholakh? Surely that creature has not taken away your courage?'

'Highness, we are searching for one man in this warren,' Sholakh protested. 'We might search for days or even weeks and still not find him.'

'I shall not leave this planet until I have that Jethryk,' the Graff stormed. 'Have you forgotten, my brave

Sholakh—our hunt for the saboteur in the Labyrinths of Knoss?'

Sholakh nodded. 'Two whole months without a glimpse of the sky,' he muttered.

'And finally a glorious success,' the Graff cried with shining eyes, staring round at his assembled Guards, impassive and silent behind their armoured masks.

'But, Highness, we had three divisions at our disposal on Knoss,' Sholakh reminded his Prince.

The Graff considered his commander's objections. 'So?' he demanded curtly.

'So we should return and force the Seeker, the Priestess, to accompany us, Highness,' Sholakh said firmly.

'Seems an excellent suggestion to me,' the Doctor remarked to himself. Lying full-length in the niche with the horn of his ear trumpet just poking round the edge of the opening, he was eavesdropping on the distant but distinguishable argument going on between the Levithian leaders. He waited impatiently for the Graff Vynda Ka's decision, knowing that with every passing second Unstoffe was getting deeper and deeper into the Catacombs with the priceless nugget.

'Very well, Sholakh,' the Levithian Prince eventually agreed. 'We shall return and compel the filthy witch to lead us—even if we have to break her legs and carry her. And if she fails, she will die.'

Cramming the battered brass trumpet back into his pocket, the Doctor peered cautiously out of the niche and saw the faint glimmer of torches as the Graff and his Guards found their way back towards the surface.

'Time I joined the Levithian Army,' he muttered, wriggling out of the narrow tomb and jumping lightly down onto the rubble strewn across the gully. He flashed his torch around, scratching his head in confusion. 'It's all right. You can all come out now,' he called. Then his eyes widened in horror.

Several of the tombs directly below his own hiding place were completely blocked by shattered masonry fallen from the tiers above. Frantically, the Doctor set to work to try and clear the huge slabs away from the openings. Somewhere beneath the mass of debris Romana, Garron and K9 were helplessly trapped inside the ancient graves. The more the Doctor struggled the more he began to fear that they would have to remain there, entombed in the vast mausoleum for ever ...

Chapter 8

The Doctor Changes Sides

As they struggled on through the maze of caverns, as quietly as they could for fear of rousing any of the Shrivenzales from their lairs, Unstoffe found himself unable to keep up with his nimble guide and eventually he sank down on a boulder, his mouth dry and his heart hammering furiously in his aching chest.

'We m-must rest ... so little ... air ...' he gasped.

Binro retraced his steps and sat down next to him. 'There *must* be a way up to the surface somewhere,' he grinned encouragingly.

Unstoffe undid his belt and set down the heavy pouch between them, glad to shed the weight for a moment.

Binro stared at his panting companion with a puzzled frown. 'How is it done? How do you run between the suns?' he asked shyly.

Unstoffe shook his head helplessly. 'If we sat here for ... for the rest of our lives, I couldn't explain,' he mumbled. Binro nodded sadly. Unstoffe reached into the pouch and pulled out the nugget of Jethryk. It gleamed brightly even in the feeble flicker of the horn lamp. 'There is enough energy in this to move us to many thousands of suns,' he murmured.

Binro took the glittering stone and gazed at it with innocent wonder. 'There is so much to learn. We on Ribos must seem like children to you,' he whispered, turning the nugget so that it reflected the lamplight in brilliant blue and silver flashes.

Unstoffe shook his head vehemently. 'Only kids would fight over a lump of rock,' he murmured.

Binro carefully handed him the Jethryk. 'You did

not steal this from the Sacred Reliquary,' he said in an awed, hushed voice.

'No, it belongs to Garron. We arranged to meet in the Concourse if anything went wrong,' Unstoffe said quietly. 'He never showed up. He's in dead trouble.'

'Garron ... the one who sent his voice through the air into your hand,' Binro guessed. Unstoffe nodded gloomily. 'You are worried about him,' Binro said, his bright eyes full of concern.

'We've worked together a long time,' Unstoffe mumbled. 'This would probably have been our last job. Only it isn't ending quite the way we planned.' He shoved the nugget away in the pouch.

Binro sprang up, his leathery little face smiling eagerly: 'I will go back and look for your friend and bring him here,' he cried. 'Then you will be able to finish your work together.'

Unstoffe peered in amazement at Binro's innocently expectant eyes: 'But ... could you find your way?' he asked, doubtfully.

Binro nodded, his wizened body tensed in readiness.

Unstoffe was baffled. 'You ... you risk your life for a complete stranger?' he stammered.

'For years I was reviled and jeered at,' Binro interrupted, 'until I even began to doubt myself. But you came and told me I was right. Just to know that is worth an old man's life.'

Binro held out his crippled hands in farewell.

'Here, take this in case Garron suspects a trick,' Unstoffe found himself saying as he slipped off his wrist transmitter and held it out. Before he realised what was happening, Binro had taken the device from him and snatched up the lamp. Unstoffe had no chance to change his mind before the elfin creature darted away and was instantly swallowed up in the darkness.

'Doctor, you realise that your clumsy behaviour nearly caused us all to be killed.'

Romana's protest startled the Doctor so badly that he let go of the heavy slab of rock he was struggling to shift and dropped it onto his foot. Hopping about grimacing with pain, he stared at the slim white figure silhouetted against the light from Garron's torch as they approached him along the gully.

'If you call that nearly getting killed, then you haven't lived,' he cried clutching his throbbing toes. Then he stood quite still and frowned at them. 'Why aren't you both dead?' he demanded irritably, picking up his flashlight and shining it in their shocked faces. 'I absolutely refuse to believe in ghosts.'

With ice-cold calmness Romana explained how she and Garron had managed to break out of the back of their niche when the opening had become blocked, and how they had escaped through the tomb on the other side into the neighbouring gully.

The Doctor smiled. 'I am delighted to see you,' he cried, 'although your unexpected resurrection almost gave me hearts' failure.'

'You appear to suffer from an unconscious death-wish syndrome, Doctor,' Romana retorted, brushing the dust out of her hair and her robe with exaggerated ferocity.

Garron thrust his ruffled perspiring bulk between them. 'May I remind you that we are supposedly searching for my invaluable young colleague?' he declared affectedly.

'Who has in his possession an even more invaluable lump of Jethryk,' the Doctor added, whipping the Locatormutor Core out of his pocket and adjusting the signal.

Garron threw up his hands and shrugged. 'What is property at such a time as this?' he protested, watching the Doctor like a hawk.

'In grave danger of giving us the slip completely if this gadget is anything to go by,' the Doctor answered, handing the bleeping Core to Romana. 'I do hope you know how to work this because I'm getting rather bored with it,' he grinned.

Taking them both firmly by the arm, the Doctor pointed his two puzzled friends in the direction of the Catacombs. 'Now you go that way and I'll go this way,' he said cheerfully, whirling round and setting off in the opposite direction back towards the city.

'But where are *you* going?' Romana asked.

The Doctor turned. 'One of us has to keep an eye on the Graff and I've just been unanimously elected,' he chuckled.

Garron shone his torch at the Doctor. 'You're going back to the city, and leaving us down here?' he exclaimed suspiciously.

The Doctor nodded impatiently. 'Well, off you go,' he cried.

There was a disjointed whirring noise and K9 trundled round a corner and ran straight into the Doctor's foot.

'And where have you been?' the Doctor demanded, staring resentfully at the creature's dusty and dented bodywork. 'No, don't even begin to tell me,' he ordered as K9's memory circuits buzzed into life. 'Just look after those two until I get back.'

'Affirmative, master,' K9 acknowledged.

With a flamboyant wave of his hat the Doctor spun round and strode off along the gully in pursuit of the Graff Vynda Ka and his retinue, without so much as a backward glance.

Romana and Garron stared at one another for a moment in utter confusion. Then Garron indicated the bleeping Locatormutor in Romana's slim white hands. 'Well, my dear,' he beamed, hitching Krolon's laser-spear and charger unit more firmly into his belt. 'Don't you think it's time we got going?'

Just as they moved off along the gully, a fierce snarling erupted from the shadows somewhere ahead of them. Romana kept her eyes firmly in front of her and walked cautiously but unflinchingly forward, leaving Garron to waddle behind her, nervously dabbing at his clammy forehead and imagining all kinds of horrors lurking in their path as they approached the unknown perils of the Catacombs . . .

In the Concourse there was an ominous silence under the dull emerald and orange dappled sky as the Graff Vynda Ka waited for the Seeker to be brought before him. The Levithian Guards in their gleaming black armour and tall helmets gripping their laser-spears in heavily gauntleted hands, were drawn up opposite the Shrieves in their clumsy fur and leather tunics grasping crude pikes and short-bladed swords. The two squads stared across at each other with mutual suspicion.

Suddenly a figure appeared bent double behind the line of hovels between the pillars of the colonnade. It sped along from hut to hut, pausing every few metres to peer into the square. It was the Doctor—his scarf wound in a fat coil up to his nose and his hat jammed low over his eyes. Just as he was about to dart across the corner of the square and into the alleyway leading to the Citadel, he saw the Captain of the Shrievalty appear under the archway. The Doctor flung himself into the nearest hovel, which luckily was empty, and peered out through a gap in the tattered skin wall.

He watched the Captain stride across to the Graff Vynda Ka.

'The Seeker will come—as soon as she has made preparations,' the Captain announced sharply.

The Graff glared at him and pulled his cloak more firmly around himself. 'An Imperial Prince should never be kept waiting,' he said in a threatening undertone.

'Gross discourtesy, Highness,' Sholakh agreed, joining them.

The Graff Vynda Ka began to tremble. The veins stood out like thongs in his temples and his neck, and he threw up his hand to try to control the violent spasms in his twitching cheek. 'Someone must be punished, Sholakh,' he screamed, snatching the laser-spear from his Commander's belt and stabbing the primer button with his armoured finger.

'Your Highness has every right to be angry,' Sholakh murmured, moving a pace or two away from his enraged master as the whine of the charger died away.

'I shall wait no longer do you hear! No longer!' the Graff shrieked pressing the discharge trigger.

There was a short sizzling burst of intense light from the barrel of the spear and one of the Shrieves crumpled to the ground with a strangled cry. For a moment the Captain of the Shrievalty stared wildly around him, unable to grasp what had happened.

'An excellent shot, Highness,' Sholakh said in congratulation.

'Not quite through the heart, I think,' the Graff muttered with a frown of irritation.

'But still an expert shot,' Sholakh said quickly, easing the laser-spear from his master's hands.

Slowly the Captain went over to the smoking body of his dead Shrieve. He stared down at the blackened hole gaping in its chest and at the rapidly welling blood spreading into the matted fur. Then he turned and pointed at the Graff Vynda Ka, stunned and speechless.

The Doctor took advantage of the diversion to creep out of his hiding place and under the archway into the surrounding alleys.

Shocked and frightened, the Captain finally managed to speak. 'You are not from the Upper Pole,' he gasped hoarsely. 'You are not ... Who ... What are you?'

'I am impatient, Captain,' the Graff snapped. 'Bring the Seeker here. Now.'

The Captain turned to his men. As he did so the air was filled with the whine of the charger units as the Levithian Guards levelled their spears at the cowering huddle of Shrieves. Some of the terrified garrison dropped their pikes and covered their eyes, while others clustered protectively around their Captain.

'Pathetic,' the Graff snorted with a cruel grin of amusement.

'Bring the Seeker,' Sholakh rapped impatiently.

Slowly the Captain backed away from them. Then he turned and hurried out of the Concourse followed closely by his Shrieves in a disorderly babbling crowd. As they straggled out through the archway the Graff turned to Sholakh with a smile of satisfaction. 'I flatter myself that I know how to handle these ignorant curs,' he muttered.

High up in the Citadel, the Doctor stared grimly down into the Concourse and watched as two terrified Shrieves made a stretcher out of their pikes and carried their dead comrade out of the square. With a frown he glanced across at the strutting figures of Sholakh and the Graff Vynda Ka, and at the neat ranks of Levithians drawn up in strict military formation in front of them.

'You need reinforcements,' he murmured. 'It's high time I changed sides.'

Flinging aside the skin curtain, the Doctor stealthily made his way along the passage to the chamber where he and his two companions had been imprisoned. He found the three sentries lying under the table where they had been dumped, still out cold. Selecting the one most similar to himself in size, he quickly began to strip off the Guard's heavy armour.

A tremendous cracking sound behind him made him freeze. Slowly he turned, his body tensed at the ready and his fingers feeling around for the controls of the charger unit and the laser-spear he had just prised out of the sentry's unconscious grip. Apart from the three slumped bodies beside him, the chamber was completely deserted.

The Doctor jumped as the crackle was repeated. A bright shower of orange sparks flared up into the chimney from a damp log in the grate. With a snort of irritation at his own nervousness the Doctor turned back to his task.

'Anybody would think I felt guilty about joining the enemy,' he muttered, his face darkening as he planned his next move ...

Clawing and spitting and shrieking curses at the top of her voice, the Seeker was dragged struggling through the Hall of the Dead, and then brutally kicked and prodded into the tunnel sloping down towards the Catacombs. There the Levithian Guards flung her to the ground and the old woman immediately sank into her customary trance.

'Soon we shall have the truth, Sholakh,' the Graff Vynda Ka muttered, 'and if the hag proves to be a charlatan you shall have her carcass for target practice.'

Sholakh nodded eagerly and then suddenly turned round. A solitary Guard was clanking towards them down the slippery tunnel from the mausoleum.

'Keep in formation there: no straggling,' Sholakh rapped frowning angrily.

The Guard halted, drew himself up smartly and slapped one gauntleted hand across to the opposite shoulder in a crisp Levithian salute. 'I was covering the rear, Commander,' he explained, his voice muffled inside the heavy metal helmet, 'just in case those Shrieve scum tried any trickery.'

Sholakh nodded with approval. 'You did well, but the cowardly vermin will not venture here.'

As the Guard clattered over to join the others in the semi-circle surrounding the silent and motionless Seeker, Sholakh watched him closely. 'I like initiative,' he smiled. 'What is your name?'

The featureless mask turned towards Sholakh and there was a moment's hesitation. Then the Guard saluted again: 'Gammon,' he replied.

Again Sholakh frowned, not recognising the name. 'Ah yes, from the Special Reserve Division?' he suggested.

'Yes, Commander.' The Guard stood stiffly to attention as the Levithian Commander looked at him for a moment before dismissing him to join the ranks.

Taking his place with the squad, the Doctor blinked the sweat out of his eyes and peered through the narrow slits in the thick armoured mask. 'So far so good,' he murmured to himself, 'though I only just saved my bacon that time.' While he watched and waited with the other Guards for the Seeker to come out of her meditation, he began to wonder how Romana and Garron were progressing deep in the heart of the labyrinth ahead.

With Garron following several metres behind covering the rear with the laser, Romana led the way through the tortuous slimy tunnels of the Catacombs illuminated starkly by the photon radiaprobe projecting from K9's muzzle like a tongue. At regular intervals she stopped to take out the Locatormutor and check the bearing on Unstoffe and the Jethryk, making the adjustments as quickly as possible in case the Core's penetrating signals should rouse a nearby Shrivenzale from its slumber.

Eventually they reached an enormous cavern with dozens of tunnels branching off in all directions. The stirrings of the invisible monsters seemed to echo eerily from everywhere at once. Romana stopped and glanced round to signal a brief halt. Garron was nowhere to be seen.

'Garron? Garron, where are you?' she called softly. There was no reply.

'Garron has departed, mistress,' K9 informed her.

Romana looked stunned. 'Departed?' she exclaimed. 'Where to?'

K9's memory circuits buzzed briefly. 'To see a man about a dog,' he announced.

'What?' Romana cried, completely nonplussed.

'That was the information Garron imparted, mistress,' K9 replied. Again his circuits buzzed. 'Three point two terrestrial minutes ago,' he added helpfully.

Romana stared at the black tunnel-mouths gaping all around the vast cavern and put her hand to her belt to take out the Locatormutor. It was not there. Frantically she searched her robe, but she found nothing. Then she glanced back in the direction they had just come, but at once realised that she would have heard it fall if it had slipped out of her belt.

'Garron must have taken the Core,' she murmured, glancing helplessly around.

'Which route now, mistress?' K9 enquired brightly.

Romana sank slowly onto a nearby boulder and looked gloomily into the robot's glowing red eyes. 'How could I have been so careless?' she murmured.

K9 tipped his head a little on one side. 'Question not understood, mistress. Please rephrase.'

Romana ignored the creature's irritating chatter. 'There is no means of locating the Segment without the Core,' she muttered, 'so what am I going to do now?'

K9's circuits began to hum furiously as he reviewed the situation at lightning speed.

'I was not asking you,' Romana snapped. 'I was talking to myself.' She was inwardly raging at Garron's sly treachery.

'Not logical,' K9 retorted briskly. 'Purpose of speech is to communicate information.'

Romana turned on the whirring mechanical hound in sheer exasperation: 'In that case be quiet until you have something useful to tell me,' she ordered angrily. K9 did not reply, but continued humming gently to himself while Romana sat silently brooding.

Eventually she turned to the Doctor's cybernetic pet with a smile of apology and asked him to advise her what to do next.

'According to previous route-patterns, we should proceed and seek in this direction,' K9 answered, setting off jerkily towards one of the tunnels on the other side of the cavern.

Glancing frequently over her shoulder, Romana followed. As K9's radiaprobe lit up the gnarled and fissured tunnel walls with their glossy, fantastically twisted surfaces resembling the fossilised remains of creatures long extinct, nightmarish sounds began to echo in the gloomy depths ahead as the hungry Shrivenzales stirred from their lairs to hunt for food ...

Unstoffe crouched on the boulder where Binro had left him, trying not to listen to the ominous stirrings of the Shrivenzales in their cavernous lairs scattered through the maze of tunnels surrounding him. Now that he had no light and not even the comfort of the miniature radio strapped to his wrist, he felt more helpless and alone than ever. He tried not to think about what would happen to him if Binro did not return for some reason.

To help pass the time he decided to count the gold opeks which jingled temptingly inside the skin purse stowed in his pouch. Fumbling in the pitch darkness he opened the fat heavy purse and dipped in his hand. The small bevelled coins ran through his fingers like grains of sand, and a shudder of excitement shook his spare little frame as he stirred the invisible treasure and listened to the thrilling chink of coin against coin.

One by one he began to transfer the gold opeks from the purse to a large pocket sewn into the lining of his furs, counting furtively under his breath: 'Eleven, twelve, thirteen ... forty-one, forty-two, forty-three ... eighty-nine, ninety, ninety-one ...' Gradually his hands moved faster and faster and his voice rose from a whisper to a breathless chanting as his pocket began to fill. And yet the purse seemed not to be emptying ...

Suddenly the boulder on which he was perched shook violently. Unstoffe stopped counting and listened. He realised that not only the boulder but the ground under his feet was beginning to vibrate with slow regular tremors. He became aware of a distant panting sound which was growing louder and nearer every second. Thrusting the purse back into his pouch, he felt his way round behind the rock and jammed himself into the narrow space between it and the cavern wall. An icy sweat broke out all over him as he shrank into the smallest possible shape and waited.

It was not long before something dragged itself ponderously into the cavern, its stentorian breath filling the air with a stale, clammy vapour as the massive lungs heaved and shuddered in the darkness. The Shrivenzale stopped only a few metres away from the cowering fugitive. Cramming his knuckles into his mouth to stop his teeth from chattering, Unstoffe prayed that the beast would not be able to sniff him out. He strained eyes and ears in a vain attempt to discover what the vast creature was doing.

A deafening crack split the air and the boulder was swept across the cavern like a golf ball as the Shrivenzale flicked its gigantic tail. Unstoffe pressed himself back against the rock wall, now utterly defenceless with nothing between him and the ravenous monster. Again the Shrivenzale lashed the cavern floor, and Unstoffe caught a momentary glimpse of its colossal armoured bulk in the light of the thick showers of sparks thrown up by the hail of jagged flints and boulders flying in all directions.

Instinctively, Unstoffe threw himself face down to dodge the deadly missiles. Then he felt the ground shudder again as the creature began to drag itself forward, and to his relief he heard it crawl away across the cavern, bellowing hungrily as it entered one of the tunnels on the far side.

Although he was in a state of considerable shock, it occurred to him that if the beast was on its way to hunt for food then it might lead him out of the Catacombs and back to the surface.

He decided to follow at a safe distance. But scarcely had he picked his way painfully across the cavern and ventured cautiously into the tunnel in the creature's wake, when he became aware of a scrambling noise behind him. When he stopped to listen the noise also stopped, resuming as soon as he set off again. Each time he looked round he thought he saw a light flicker and then go out, leaving a faint pinkish glow that seemed to pulse in time to a strange high-pitched bleeping.

'Must be hallucinating,' he muttered. All the same he groped around and armed himself with a chunk of flint before creeping onwards in pursuit of the Shrivenzale. It seemed that this terrible beast might well give him his only chance of escaping from the endless labyrinth. But as he crept cautiously forward he began to realise that if there really was something behind him, then he would be helplessly trapped, with no chance of escape.

Chapter 9

Lost and Found

At last the Seeker emerged from her trance and uttering her weird chant, she cast the bones onto the slimy
floor of the tunnel and studied their alignment.

'I see him. The one you seek is near,' she cried. But
then she clutched her temples and began to sway round
and round like a reed in the wind. 'We shall never
reach him,' she murmured her voice cracking like dry
sticks. 'I see Death standing between.'

Sholakh prodded her viciously with his laser-spear.
'Death is standing right here, sorceress,' he snarled, 'so
lead on.'

Snatching up her bones the Seeker held them in her
outstretched claws and raked the semi-circle of metal-
masked figures with her crazed eyes. 'I will lead you
if that is your wish,' she rasped in a spine-chilling
whisper. 'But take good heed. All but one of us are
doomed to die. All but one.'

There was an uneasy stir among the Guards. Several
of the faceless masks turned to one another in unspoken
alarm.

Sholakh paced angrily up and down the ranks.
'What are you?' he growled. 'Crack commandos of his
Highness's Imperial Guard—or trembling Shrieves
frightened by the spells of their so-called priestess?'

'Well, some of us might not be quite what we seem,'
the Doctor murmured to himself, standing stiffly to
attention inside his cumbersome armour.

Sholakh stopped directly in front of him, gazing
intently into the eye slits of the Guard's heavy vizor.
'What was that?' he barked.

The Doctor gave him a stylish salute. 'We shall follow his Highness to the end, Commander,' he said crisply.

Sholakh nodded. 'A fine example,' he announced to the other Guards. Then he ordered the squad into marching formation and prodded the Seeker forward into the Catacombs.

Unstoffe soon realised that he was not hallucinating at all. The strangely flashing light, the eerie pinkish glow and the sinister bleeping were real enough: something was stalking him and coming closer every second. Forgetting about the Shrivenzale lumbering towards the surface ahead of him, he wriggled into a narrow crack in the tunnel wall, held his breath and listened.

The persistent bleeping had merged into a sustained high-pitched whine and a steady pink aura began to flood the tunnel. Whatever it was, his pursuer could not be more than a dozen metres away. Unstoffe raised the chunk of flint above his head, his mind invaded by terrible images of Ice Gods and ancient alien demons.

Suddenly the whining sound stopped and everything went dark. Unstoffe tensed like a spring as a curious shuffling noise approached through the blackness. There was also a muffled asthmatic breathing which was somehow familiar, but Unstoffe had no time to think. He drew back his arms ...

Before he could strike something sank heavily onto his foot. He yelped with pain and fright like a trampled puppy.

'If I ain't standing on your foot, my son, this gadget has to be Japanese,' hissed a familiar voice.

Unstoffe dropped the flint as a welcome torchbeam flashed over his pinched features. 'Garron!' he cried. 'Am I glad to see you!'

'Likewise, my dear,' Garron replied, surveying his

trembling accomplice.

'But how did you find me?' Unstoffe asked in astonishment.

Garron waved the Locatormutor Core under his nose. 'The wonders of modern technology,' he beamed. 'I just happened to come across this handy little electronic bloodhound. Sniffs Jethryk like a dream.' Garron thrust the Core into his belt and directed his torch at Unstoffe's bulging pouch.

'Do I hear the chink of the Graff's gold?' he grinned, ripping open the flap and staring hungrily at the contents of the heavy leather bag.

'Listen, mate, first things first,' Unstoffe began, still suffering from shock and anxious to find a way of escaping from the underground warren.

'Just what I always say,' Garron muttered, picking out the Jethryk and watching it flash and sparkle. 'I'm very attached to this.'

'Listen, money isn't everything, you know,' Unstoffe exploded, 'and right now we ought to be ...'

'So who wants *everything*?' Garron interrupted, pulling out the pouch and shaking it in his face. 'I'll settle for ninety per cent, my son—*any* day.'

After recounting his own exploits at some length and with certain embellishments, Garron listened to Unstoffe's account of his escape helped by Binro with sceptical amusement.

'You really believe he'll come back down here?' he chuckled cynically.

'I know he will,' Unstoffe retorted, 'after he's risked his life scouring the city to find you.'

'That'll take him hours,' Garron said in a suddenly chastened tone, shining his torch up and down the tunnel with an uneasy frown. 'Let's hope the Graff doesn't get to us first. He's press-ganged some old hag to sniff us out.'

For a while neither of them spoke.

'What about this Doctor bloke and the girl?' Unstoffe suddenly burst out. 'Perhaps they'll find us.'

'Not without this they won't, I'm glad to say,' Garron muttered, patting the Locatormutor Core stuck in his belt.

Unstoffe looked genuinely shocked. 'They helped you escape and you stole that from them,' he cried.

Garron regarded his outraged apprentice with condescending sternness. 'They were temporary allies in adversity, my lad,' he shrugged. 'And I wouldn't trust 'em further than I could fling 'em.'

'What's happened to them now?' Unstoffe demanded.

Garron waved his podgy hands dismissively. 'The Doctor went off to spy on the Graff—or so he said— and the girl's wandering about down here somewhere.'

Unstoffe stared in utter disgust. 'Down here? Alone?' he exclaimed. 'You just nicked the whatsis-name and then left her?'

'Oh I am quite sure that Madam can take care of herself,' Garron retorted in a refined voice.

Unstoffe broke angrily away. 'How could you,' he cried, 'you slimy old hypocrite.'

At once Garron's practised ears caught the faint jingle of coins. Training his torch on Unstoffe's pale ferret-like face, he advanced on him and plunged his hands into the lining of his young associate's furs.

'I do admit I had an epic struggle with my *con- science*,' he hissed, seizing the hundred or so gold opeks Unstoffe had counted out earlier. 'But unfortunately, my lad, *I* won.' Garron poured the coins into the purse he was holding and then grabbed Unstoffe by the collar.

'I . . . I can explain,' Unstoffe stammered. 'I was only counting them to check . . .' He knew Garron would never believe him.

'I ought to skin you alive, my lad,' Garron growled, shaking Unstoffe like a leaf in a gale. 'Make no mistake, when we get out of here I'll . . .'

Garron's threat was cut short by a titanic bellow which tore suddenly through the tunnel. Garron dropped his torch which smashed to pieces and clung to Unstoffe like a frightened child in the dark.

'You'll what?' breathed Unstoffe mockingly in his boss's ear. 'Come on Godfather. What will you do?'

'I'll ... I'll see you get your rightful share, my boy,' Garron stuttered clinging on for dear life.

Unstoffe listened a moment. 'It's the one I was following,' he whispered. 'It's coming back. It must have smelt you, Garron.' And he started to drag the terrified Garron back along the tunnel towards the cavern where he had first encountered the Shrivenzale, as the voracious beast thundered closer and closer...

As he marched forward with the other Levithian Guards, the Doctor kept careful watch on the Seeker through the eye slits of his helmet as she led the Graff Vynda Ka and his retinue through the Catacombs, the bones gripped in her outstretched hands seeming to twist and turn with a power all their own. He was trying to decide whether the wizened crone did indeed possess special powers, or whether she was merely a crafty charlatan leading them all to their deaths.

Suddenly Sholakh ordered them to halt. 'Over there, Highness, something moved.' He pointed to a cluster of massive fallen rocks strewn around the huge cavern they had just entered.

The Guards trained their lasers on the spot where Binro was cowering, dazzled by the torches. Two of them seized the sinewy little figure and flung him at the feet of the Graff.

'What are you doing here?' the Prince demanded as the Guards jerked back Binro's head by the strands of his grey hair.

'Looking for fossils, sir,' Binro croaked. 'Just fossils.'

'Grave robbing more likely,' the Graff snarled,

slashing at the old man's face with his gauntlets as he tried vainly to shield his watering eyes from the cruel glare.

The Doctor gritted his teeth and forced himself to remain silent inside the borrowed armour.

'I sell the fossils, sir,' Binro pleaded. 'I cannot work ... my hands are crippled.'

Sholakh reached down and forced open Binro's tightly clenched hand. Behind his anonymous mask the Doctor's eyes widened as he saw Unstoffe's wrist radio clatter to the ground.

'A rare fossil indeed,' the Graff murmured as Sholakh handed him the tiny device. 'Where did you get this?' he demanded with a vicious kick at the frail figure crouching in front of him.

'I found it, sir,' Binro mumbled, flinching away from the young Prince's heavy boot.

Sholakh shoved his laser-spear against Binro's wrinkled brow. 'The truth, or I'll blast your head off,' he snapped.

But the Graff Vynda Ka held up his hand imperiously and stared thoughtfully at the miniature radio. 'Bring him,' he ordered, and spurred the Seeker onwards with a flick of his gloves.

The two Guards yanked Binro off the ground and joined ranks, dragging the helpless old man between them like a sack.

'We seem to be getting warmer at last,' the Doctor murmured to himself, blinking the sweat out of his eyes and peering intently at the wizened little figure dangling pathetically in the cruel grip of his two enormous captors.

For some time Romana had been following K9 through the endless tunnels and caverns, inwardly fuming at Garron's audacious trickery and her own carelessness.

'I am certain that we have been this way before,' she

complained wearily, 'it all looks very familiar.' She was becoming less and less confident of K9's sense of direction.

'Affirmative and Negative, mistress,' the robot replied buzzing busily ahead.

Romana stopped, hands planted firmly on hips. 'Whatever do you mean?' she demanded, staring with sinking heart at the maze of branching tunnels in the light of K9's radiaprobe.

'We have traversed this section twice previously, but my scanners detect many differences,' came the prompt, mechanical announcement as the Doctor's pet ground to a halt.

Romana glared. 'Do you think I enjoy walking round in circles?' she snapped. The robot was almost as infuriating as his master.

K9 considered for a moment. 'Enjoyment is a humanoid emotion,' he rasped. 'My circuits are not programmed to analyse the condition.'

Romana threw up her hands. 'Don't lecture me, K9. Just indicate a route we have not already covered,' she pleaded.

K9 swivelled his antennae obligingly and jerked abruptly into motion.

'It is so frustrating to have to rely on inferior equipment,' Romana said to herself as she followed her whirring guide into yet another warren of identical tunnels in their seemingly hopeless quest.

Suddenly, K9 jerked to a halt a few paces ahead of her with a curt warning, 'Danger, mistress,' and Romana quickly flattened herself against the tunnel wall.

She waited apprehensively while the mechanical hound buzzed away analysing something he had detected. Then she too heard it: a heavily rhythmic breathing coming from a few metres round the bend ahead of them.

K9 began to reverse, trundling past her and backing away up the tunnel.

'What is it K9? Where are you going?' Romana whispered in a panic.

'Tone analysis indicates large carnivore. Species unidentified. Intentions hostile,' he replied quietly, spinning round and retreating rapidly back the way they had just come.

Romana pulled herself together and caught up, glancing repeatedly over her shoulder as she ran. 'But you can't be afraid—fear is an emotion,' she murmured. 'So why are you running away?'

Just then a gigantic roar shuddered through the tunnel and Romana felt a hot clammy draught on the back of her neck.

'Suggest mistress arranges immediate protection for her circuitry,' K9 advised as he juddered along beside her.

The ponderous leathery scrabbling sounds gained on them as the Shrivenzale smelt a meal within its grasp and forced its way through the tunnel, its claws and scales shrieking as they scoured the jagged rocky surface in its wake.

As the frustrated roars of the approaching Shrivenzale rang around the cavern, Garron fumbled in the pitch darkness and drew the laser-spear out of his belt. 'I wonder how this little trinket works,' he muttered breathlessly, his fingers groping frantically among the controls bristling from its slim barrel.

'Ssssssh,' Unstoffe suddenly hissed, dragging Garron back into a deep fissure he had located behind them. 'I see lights.'

Seconds later the blackness was criss-crossed by a dozen sharp torchbeams as the Seeker led the Graff Vynda Ka and his men into the cavern. The Seeker clutched the bones to her forehead and then stretched them in front of her to form the point of a spear, moving her arms in slow circles as if feeling for the exact spot where the quarry lay.

'The one you seek is here,' she breathed. The sweeping torchbeams probed a cluster of rocks by the cavern wall. Garron and Unstoffe shrank back as the lights blazed around them.

'No ... No, it was this way ... this way ...' Binro screamed, abruptly tearing free from his captors and scrambling towards one of the gaping tunnel mouths scattered round the cavern walls.

'Hold him,' Sholakh ordered, his eyes still fixed on the cluster of rocks pointed out by the Seeker.

'Unstoffe! Run ... Run ...' Binro shrieked, ducking and swerving around the centre of the cavern.

Unstoffe leapt out of his hiding place just as a searing volley of photon bolts burst from the humming laser-spears and blew away almost the whole of one side of Binro's frail body. He caught his dying friend and lowered him gently to the ground.

Binro's eyes stared wildly. He struggled to speak. Unstoffe just managed to catch a few faintly gasped words: 'Binro, the ... Heretic ... truth ...'

'Yes, Binro was right. He told the truth,' Unstoffe murmured, averting his gaze from the limp remains of Binro's charred body.

Within seconds the old man was dead. Unstoffe sprang up and reached across to grab the laser-spear from the cowering Garron. 'Murderers!' he screamed, pointing the unfamiliar weapon crazily at the Levithians on the other side of the cavern who were priming their own lasers with a sinister whine. A burst of photon beams ricocheted off a nearby boulder sending splinters of rock slicing in all directions. Clutching his shoulder, Unstoffe dropped the laser-spear and collapsed whimpering with terror. A few seconds later Garron emerged from the crevice with his arms raised high in surrender.

As Garron advanced towards the Levithians dazzled by the merciless torchlight, there was a sudden muffled cracking and grating sound from the cavern roof followed by a hail of rock fragments and dust.

'Quick, over here!' Sholakh yelled, glancing fearfully upwards as he rallied his forces into a less exposed position.

Garron helped his shocked and wounded associate to his feet and supported him as they scrambled across the huge cavern to the waiting Guards. A fine rain of dust was falling and the roof creaked threateningly overhead.

'Binro warned me about the roofs down here,' Unstoffe gasped. As he spoke a thick slab of rock about a metre square flew past them and shattered into tiny splinters. In the stark torchlight a long crack was gradually beginning to open above them.

'The Jethryk ... Where is the Jethryk?' the Graff Vynda Ka cried immediately as they approached him and were quickly surrounded.

Garron unfastened the pouch from his belt and handed it to Sholakh. 'You will find everything quite safe, Your Highness,' he murmured humbly with a slight bow.

Sholakh opened the leather flap and the Graff Vynda Ka's eyes burned with triumph as he feasted them on the glinting nugget and the purse bulging with gold opeks within. 'Excellent, Sholakh, excellent,' he purred. 'Now we have all that we want, at last.'

Then he turned his pale fanatical gaze upon the perspiring Garron and his injured accomplice. 'And now all that remains is the disposal of these petty criminals,' he sneered. 'Where are your other associates?'

Garron frowned. 'Other associates, Highness?' he echoed in a puzzled tone.

The Graff raised his bunched gauntlets in a white-knuckled hand ready to strike. 'Do not play with the Graff Vynda Ka,' he snarled. 'Where are they?'

'Ah yes of course—Your Highness is no doubt referring to the two Alliance Security Agents,' Garron hastily went on with an ingratiating smile. 'They had just arrested me for landing and trading without a licence when Your Highness saw fit to betray his presence: very heavy-handed if you will pardon my saying so ...'

The armoured gauntlets slashed through the air: 'You lie! You lie!' the Graff screamed.

But the burly con-man neatly sidestepped the vicious blow and chattered on. 'Why should I bother?' he beamed smugly. 'Their report will reach the Alliance any moment and then you will no longer be a Prince of the Cyrrhenic Empire and a conquering hero—you'll be a common criminal just like us.'

For a full minute the Graff could only utter incoherent and meaningless exclamations. Then he stamped away to a safe distance waving his arms at his assembled Guards. 'Execute ... Execute them!' he shrieked through pale frothing lips.

Instantly the Levithians formed themselves into a firing squad. During Garron's exchange with the raging Prince, the Doctor had managed to manoeuvre the dog whistle out of his trouser pocket and blow an urgent summons to K9. He was just shoving the whistle back through the join in his borrowed armour when he saw the Graff glance suspiciously at him. Hurriedly he took up his position and charged his laser.

But it was too late. Already the Graff Vynda Ka was striding towards him with gauntlets raised. 'Why are you so slow?' the Graff screamed frenziedly, ignoring Garron's insolent smile as he clung to his dazed accomplice in front of the humming laser-spears.

The entire execution squad turned to stare at their reprimanded comrade. But before the Doctor could speak a gargantuan Shrivenzale burst out of one of the tunnels and scuttled into the centre of the cavern, sparks crackling from its scrabbling claws and from its lashing tail. As its deafening roars rocked the huge subterranean vault, deep fissures opened up and spread in all directions with ear-splitting detonations. The roof of the cavern began to buckle and disintegrate, hurling showers of jagged splinters down onto the flailing beast.

Sholakh strode forward yelling the order to stand firm and counter-attack. In the pandemonium Garron and Unstoffe were forgotten as the Levithians discharged fusillade after fusillade at the savage reptilian monster bearing down on them, its jaws scything and gnashing with each lunge of its dragon's head. Thick clouds of acrid black smoke filled the cavern as the creature's hide began to melt under the relentless bombardment, and dust and rocks flew everywhere as the shuddering roof broke up.

The Graff Vynda Ka seemed immune from danger as he stood among his Guards screaming orders and gesturing defiantly with clenched gauntlets at the raging beast. Around him the cries of the Levithians were barely audible in the uproar as they were seized in twos and threes and mangled in the Shrivenzale's merciless jaws, before being tossed like rag-dolls to lie smashed and trampled in the semi-darkness.

Eventually the Shrivenzale began to retreat, dragging itself from under the colossal slabs of falling rock, its hide a twisted tacky mess of molten and perforated scales and one of its huge eyes reduced to a smouldering blackened crater. As it backed away towards the tunnel, Sholakh rallied his gravely depleted ranks, their arms shaken by the throbbing lasers and their armour ripped and battered into scrap. When at last the beast had disappeared and all that remained was the raucous echo of its whimpering, scarcely half a dozen guards were left to cluster faithfully round their Commander and their Prince.

Not far away, Romana was listening to the nearby battle while the tunnel creaked around her like the ropes and timbers of a ship in a gale, and it seemed to her as if the entire Catacombs were undergoing some cataclysmic upheaval. The tunnel was filling with smoke and dust and despite K9's powerful radiaprobe beam, she could hardly see more than a metre or two in front of her.

'What is happening?' she shouted, brushing the grit out of her watering eyes and choking on the thick fumes.

'I detect considerable seismic activity, mistress,' K9 replied faintly.

Romana immediately groped her way towards the metallic voice. 'I know that,' she cried impatiently. 'But what is causing it?'

Suddenly she found herself flying through the air. She landed heavily on the vibrating floor of the tunnel and stared up into K9's softly glowing eyes. 'Why did you stop?' she demanded rubbing her badly chafed shins.

'In order to reconcile our respective velocities, mistress,' K9 replied smartly.

Romana scrambled painfully to her feet. 'I am perfectly capable of keeping up with you,' she retorted.

'Negative, mistress . . .' K9 began to argue.

'Don't contradict me, just tell me what is . . .' Romana was cut short by a deafening whiplash. The tunnel suddenly started to twist and buckle, throwing them violently around.

Covering her head with her arms, Romana crouched against the metal casing of K9 as sharp splinters and small boulders began to fly around them. Gradually larger and larger sections of the tunnel collapsed with a grinding roar, and it seemed that it would be only a matter of seconds before they were buried beneath a torrent of shattered rock . . .

As soon as Sholakh had given the order to ceasefire he rushed over to the Graff Vynda Ka who was still standing like a statue, oblivious of any danger, his fanatical gaze fixed on the tunnel into which the Shrivenzale had retreated.

'Back, Highness! Back!' he cried, grabbing his master's arm and pointing to the groaning roof above them.

'Victory, Sholakh. A glorious victory,' the Graff murmured, turning to his Commander with mad, glazed eyes. 'And this is but the beginning ...'

'The roof, Highness,' Sholakh yelled, desperately dragging the Levithian Prince towards the safety of one of the tunnel mouths where the Seeker was kneeling, her arms and head thrown back and her face a macabre grinning mask.

Just as Sholakh pushed his master into the protection of the tunnel entrance, the roof of the cavern collapsed with a roar and he was pinned helplessly under a huge slab of rock. In the choking darkness, pierced only by one or two pencils of light from torches dropped by the half-buried Guards, screams rang out and then died away. Then a threatening silence filled the shattered cavern.

Desperately the Graff Vynda Ka struggled to free Sholakh, but he could not budge the massive slab. Sholakh twisted his body from side to side in agony, desperately trying to speak.

'No ... no, Highness ... Leave me ... Leave me ...' he moaned.

'Never, Sholakh, never,' the Graff murmured, re-doubling his futile efforts. 'You have never deserted me, Sholakh. I shall never desert you.'

Sholakh spat the welling blood out of his mouth. 'Highness ... the Jethryk ... the Jethryk ...' he croaked, his eyes rolling and his hands shaking in violent spasms.

'Ah yes, the Jethryk ...' the Graff breathed hoarsely, feverishly yanking at the clips securing one of the pouches to Sholakh's belt. The Levithian Commander shuddered in pain as his master roughly worked the pouch out from under his crushed legs.

No sooner had the Graff freed it than he spun round at a sudden movement behind him. One of his crack Levithian Guards stood there at attention.

'Here . . . help me,' he ordered. The Guard marched forward.

'It is too late,' the Seeker croaked from the shadows. 'Sholakh is dead.'

With a gasp the Graff dropped the heavy pouch and turned back to his faithful Commander: Sholakh's eyes stared unseeingly up at him.

While the Graff knelt there with his head bowed in silent grief, the Guard quietly picked up the pouch and opening it, checked that the nugget of Jethryk was indeed intact. Then with deftly rapid movements he closed the pouch and waited.

With a sigh the Graff roused himself from his brief vigil. Gently he prised open Sholakh's hand and removed the purse containing the one million gold opeks from his death grasp. Slowly he rose to his feet.

'We shall avenge you, Sholakh,' he cried dramatically, raising his hand in farewell. 'We shall bombard this filthy planet until nothing remains to show that it ever existed . . .'

With that the Graff Vynda Ka motioned the Guard to accompany him. He gave the grinning Seeker a sharp kick: 'Lead us back to the Hall of the Dead,' he shouted, sending her scrambling into the tunnel ahead of them.

Watching the Graff's every move through the narrow eye slits of his helmet, the Doctor marched stiffly beside the Levithian Prince, clutching the pouch containing the Jethryk tightly under his arm. Whenever he had the chance, he took out the dog whistle and blew a hurried blast unnoticed by the Graff. At last the Segment was in his possession, or so he hoped. But what had happened to Romana and K9?

Chapter 10

Conjuring Tricks

On the far side of the enormous cavern beyond the massive rock-fall from the roof, two dust-covered figures lay huddled. After a long time one of them stirred and uttering exaggerated groans began to tug at the limp arm of his companion.

'Come on, Garron. Come on,' Unstoffe urged, stumbling in the jagged debris scattered around them.

The bulky prostrate figure opened its eyes. 'Am I dead yet?' Garron enquired plaintively.

Unstoffe managed to drag his portly associate upright. Garron gave an agonised moan and hopped about dramatically.

'Lousy shots ... they got me in the foot,' he whimpered.

Unstoffe clutched his own injured shoulder. 'I'm the one who got shot at,' he retorted. 'You just got trodden on by a falling pebble when the roof fell in.'

Garron stood still and stared around. 'Oh, is that all?' he exclaimed sarcastically. 'So now we're buried alive, eh?'

Unstoffe nodded despairingly.

Garron pulled the Locatormutor Core out of his belt. 'I think I'd rather be dead, my boy,' he muttered gloomily. 'Do you think we could commit suicide with this gadget?'

Unstoffe suddenly motioned him to be quiet. They listened. Faint knocking sounds were coming from a huge mound of rocks where one of the tunnel mouths had been blocked by the roof-fall. Unstoffe seized a small boulder and, gritting his teeth against the pain in his shoulder, began to beat on the jagged stones, stopping every few seconds to listen for any sign of a response.

Trapped in the blocked tunnel, Romana was struggling to clear a way through the mass of fallen rock, but she was unable to budge even the smallest of the jagged lumps of flint. Her lungs bursting with the effort and her hands stinging with painful gashes from the sharp stones, she soon gave up the hopeless task. She slumped wearily against the buckled tunnel wall and wiped the thick dust out of her eyes and mouth.

'It's no good K9. There's no way we can get through,' she murmured in despair.

Just then there was a faint but unmistakable knocking sound. Romana held her breath. K9 swivelled his antennae in the direction of the regular tapping and then trundled quickly up to the rock-fall.

'Protect your audio-receptors, mistress,' he advised her.

Romana backed away and put her hands up over her ears as requested. The bright light emitted by K9's radiaprobe suddenly dimmed to a faint glow, and a piercing high-pitched whine ripped through the gloom. Romana felt a sickening, rapid throbbing begin to pulse relentlessly through her body and the sensation became so violent that she feared she would be shaken to pieces. She opened her mouth to cry out but the vibrating air stifled her like an invisible gag.

With a soundless scream she crashed to the ground in a dead faint as K9's powerful ultrasonic beam split the mass of rock asunder and quickly reduced it to a huge heap of shingle.

Garron and Unstoffe looked on in amazement as the gigantic mound of rock by the cavern wall gradually disintegrated into small fragments. They were even more astonished when a few moments later, Romana appeared through the settling dust and crunched down the shingly slope towards them.

'Ah, there you are, my dear,' Garron beamed, 'I can't tell you how delighted I am to see you again.

I've been searching everywhere for you and ...' Garron paused and followed Romana's icy stare down to the Locatormutor Core he was still holding. 'I wanted to give you this,' he went on with oily politeness. 'You dropped it.'

Romana smiled coldly. 'You know, you could be extremely useful in the slips,' she retorted, easing the Core out of Garron's clammy grasp. She switched it on and held it out in front of her, turning slowly in a circle until she found the position which produced the most continuous signals.

The direction indicated lay over the mound of pulverised rock and back into the tunnel where Romana had been trapped and where K9 was patiently waiting for her.

'The First Segment ...' Romana breathed, starting back over the shifting mound towards the tunnel.

Garron waddled forward clearing his throat noisily. 'Let me carry that for you. You look rather pale and faint, my dear,' he proposed. Unstoffe cast his eyes upward in despair at Garron's lack of subtlety and nudged his associate sharply.

Romana totally ignored them and disappeared over the top of the mound of pulverised rock into the tunnel beyond, leaving the two indignant swindlers to scramble awkwardly and anxiously after her.

In the innermost depths of the Hall of the Dead, surrounded by the bones of their ancestors, the Shrieves had set up a huge ancient cannon so that its gaping muzzle pointed directly at the entrance to the Catacomb labyrinth. The Captain of the Shrievalty barked orders continuously as he supervised the loading of the primitive but enormous weapon with boulders and heavy iron projectiles. When the sweating nervous Shrieves had rammed the shot tightly into position, he personally primed the touch hole with powder and then made final adjustments to the aim and range, sighting carefully along the thick ornate barrel.

'It is said that no one ever returns from the depths of the Catacombs,' he said solemnly to the assembled Shrieves when he had completed the preparations. 'Now we shall make sure of it—by sealing them for ever...'

After a final check, the Captain took a flaring brand from one of his men and made ready to light the fuse...

As the Seeker led the way back towards the Hall of the Dead, the Graff Vynda Ka raved and threatened in a crazed obsessive voice, vowing total destruction of the planet Ribos to the Doctor marching silently at his side. When at last they came in sight of the narrow funnel of rock which formed the entrance to the labyrinth, the Graff halted. He stared at the cringing old woman with maddened eyes. Searching among the folds of his cape he drew out a pair of small ceremonial daggers with elaborately carved handles and slim flashing blades.

The Graff raised the daggers aloft in imitation of the Seeker's ritualistic gestures with her bones. 'What is the prophecy?' he cried hysterically. 'All but one doomed to die?'

The grinning hag nodded gleefully.

'Then die!' he shrieked, plunging the knives deep into the Seeker's scrawny body.

The Doctor looked on uneasily as the gaping wounds showed not the slightest trace of bleeding. Flourishing her bones defiantly the Seeker uttered a spine-chilling cackle and stumbled wildly away towards the Hall of the Dead.

The Graff Vynda Ka watched impassively as the mortally wounded priestess staggered out of sight in the harsh white light from the Doctor's torch. Then he turned to the one remaining member of his crack Levithian Guard.

'And now the most glorious task falls to you—the very last of my Invincibles,' he cried. 'Were you with me in the Skarrno Campaign?'

'No, Your Highness, I did not have that great honour,' came the Doctor's muffled reply as he watched the Graff slowly pulling off his armoured gauntlets.

The Graff reached out and began to make rapid adjustments to the complex network of connections on top of the charger unit clipped to the Doctor's belt.

'So many honours . . . so many victories . . .' he raved as he swiftly reconnected the terminals. 'I remember Sholakh planting my Imperial Standard right in the very heart of the Skarrnoest Emperor. And now Sholakh too is dead . . .'

The adjustments completed, the Graff pulled on his gauntlets and reached out for the pouch containing the Jethryk nugget. The Doctor handed it over.

The Graff stepped back clipping the pouch firmly onto his belt. 'All but one is doomed to die,' he murmured, glancing down at the charger unit at the Doctor's side. 'And it will be the highest honour for you to sacrifice yourself in the service of the Graff Vynda Ka—and to seal the tomb of your beloved Commander Sholakh for ever.'

The Graff stepped forward again and embraced the last of his Levithians with solemn ceremony. As he did so, the Doctor deftly removed the charger unit from his own belt and with lightning fingers exchanged it for the lump of Jethryk in the pouch. Then, holding the precious nugget behind his back, he performed a smart salute with his free hand in reply to the Graff's farewell.

'Ladies and gentlemen, there is absolutely nothing up my sleeves,' the Doctor murmured to himself as he watched the Graff turn and stride quickly away towards the Hall of the Dead. Then he began hurriedly searching along the walls of the tunnel for a suitable place to take cover . . .

*　　*　　*

135

Just as the Shrieve Captain thrust the flaring brand into the touch hole of the massive cannon, the Seeker dragged herself into the entrance to the echoing necropolis from the Catacombs. The Captain shielded his face and stared in horror between his fingers as the old woman lurched to a stop in front of the mighty gun. Flinging up her fragile arms she released the sacred bones so that they smashed into the tunnel roof as the powder sizzled in the fuse hole. The brittle fragments rattled around her as she stared into the gaping muzzle of the cannon.

'All ... but ... one ...' she shrieked.

With a stunning roar the cannon fired, its massive bulk hurled backwards by the recoil. The Seeker disappeared in the fireball of rock and shrapnel which tore into the tunnel and instantly destroyed the only entrance to the Catacombs with a noise like thunder.

In the long silence which followed, the Captain and his Shrieves stood in the smoke-filled mausoleum, their heads bowed in tribute to their dead priestess. Then the Captain raised his head and nodded grimly.

'No one has ever returned,' he murmured, 'and now no one ever shall.'

The Graff Vynda Ka stood in the entrance to what remained of the tunnel leading out of the Catacombs, his whole body trembling uncontrollably and his eyes seared by the ferocious blast from the Shrieves' cannon. He was snatching his breath in short hysterical gasps between tightly clenched teeth, and all over his face and neck the blue veins bulged like whipcords. He stared fixedly but blindly in the direction of the avalanche blocking the way back into the Hall of the Dead, and eventually began to mutter under his breath.

Soon his muttering grew to a shout and then to a screaming refrain as he flung back his head with a final mad rallying cry. 'To me my Invincibles ... To me ... To me ...' he shrieked in a blind frenzy. Brandishing the pouch into which Sholakh had put the

Jethryk, he lowered his head and threw himself into the blocked tunnel like a charging bull.

The Doctor jammed his cumbersome armour-plated body as best he could into a crevice in the wall at the other end of the tunnel. 'Ten ... nine ... eight ...' he murmured, listening intently through his thick metal helmet to the Graff's crazed voice echoing in the tunnel. 'To me, Sholakh. To me. Cover the flank there. Charge ...'

'Four ... three ... two ... one ...' The Doctor counted, gripping the nugget of Jethryk anxiously in his gloved hands.

There was a brief silence. Then a blinding flash momentarily lit up the tunnel and there was a colossal explosion. The Doctor was brushed out of the crevice as if by some gigantic paw, and hurled down the tunnel into the first of the caverns forming the labyrinth of the Catacombs. He lay quite still. As the echoing detonation died away he heard a curious tinkling sound all around him. Then complete silence, except for an insistent ringing inside his head from the stunning force of the explosion.

Eventually the Doctor clambered slowly and painfully to his feet and thankfully removed the heavy stifling helmet from his shoulders. In the bright circle of light from his torch he saw that he was completely surrounded by a thin carpet of small gold coins. 'Pennies from heaven?' he mused, bending down awkwardly to pick one up. As he stared at the dully gleaming opek, embossed with the crest of the Cyrrhenic Imperial Exchequer, it occurred to the Doctor that perhaps the thousands and thousands of coins should be collected and returned to the Imperial Chancellor.

But with a shrug he flicked the coin away into the darkness. 'All that glitters ...' he muttered, quickly releasing the clamps securing his armour and wriggling free from the cumbrous metal suit. He pulled his hat out of his coat pocket, thumped it into shape and stuck it carelessly on his head with a huge sigh of relief.

Suddenly the Doctor frowned. He stared down at his empty hands. Then he rummaged quickly through his bulging pockets. 'All that glitters ... is not gold,' he cried, anxiously shining the torch beam round the cavern floor, 'and I've been robbed!'

Frantically he began to stride round the cavern shining the torch all over its vast, rock-strewn floor and kicking the gleaming gold opeks angrily aside. At last he came back to the heap of Levithian armour lying where he had shed it. In a furious outburst he kicked it and sent it clattering into the shadows. There at his feet lay the nugget of Jethryk glittering brilliantly in the torchlight.

'Eureka!' he cried, snatching it up and examining it closely. It seemed to be intact. He wrapped it carefully in his vast spotted handkerchief and thrust it deep into his overcoat.

The Doctor's broad smile of delight at finding the Jethryk again immediately faded to a frown of apprehension as he set off across the cavern in the direction of the tunnel where the Graff Vynda Ka had been blown to pieces. 'All but one is doomed to die,' he murmured as he passed the discarded armour huddled among the rocks. 'And the question is—which one?' After a few paces he raised the torch and shone it along the tunnel, hardly daring to look to see if there remained any possible escape route.

In a few seconds he would discover whether the blast from the charger unit had cleared a way through the avalanche made by the Shrieves, or whether he was doomed to be an eternal prisoner of the ancient labyrinth ...

Scarf ends flying, his hat at a rakish angle and his face one huge smile, the Doctor breezed through the archway of the city gate closely followed by Romana, K9, Garron and Unstoffe.

'Oh, ask me anything,' he cried cheerfully, 'anything you like. Which came first the chicken or the egg? Anything...'

Garron was shaking his head in admiration as he hurried along. 'But how did you switch the charger unit for the Jethryk without the Graff noticing?' he asked.

The Doctor shrugged. 'Oh, sleight of hand you know,' he called over his shoulder. 'Just the usual old tricks, Garron.'

Garron exchanged a significant glance with his breathless associate and tapped the side of his nose craftily.

'I suppose that it was quite a clever move,' Romana conceded in an off-hand voice.

'Quite clever?' the Doctor exclaimed, stopping abruptly so that the others had some difficulty avoiding cannoning into one another. 'Quite clever? It was a stroke of sheer genius,' he protested, turning to them and holding up the spotted handkerchief containing the precious nugget. 'If I had not succeeded,' he went on sternly, 'not only would the Segment have fallen into the wrong hands—possibly with dire consequences for the entire Universe—but none of us would be here now.'

After a short silence Garron came up to the Doctor, his beady eyes full of respect. 'We are all eternally grateful, Doctor,' he beamed, 'but I have one last favour to request—the Jethryk—if I might be permitted to hold it for a moment? One last look?'

To Romana's horror the Doctor readily handed the bulging handkerchief to the fawning con-man, and turned unconcernedly away to clear the drifted snow piled against the door of the barely visible TARDIS.

Beaming with pleasure, Garron stood in the pale green sunlight stroking the nugget lovingly. 'You cannot imagine how reluctant I am to part with it,' he murmured.

The Doctor unlocked the door of the TARDIS and

pushed it open. 'Oh, I think I can, Garron,' he grinned turning round with outstretched hand.

Reluctantly, Garron wrapped up the colourful bundle and gave it back. 'So this is goodbye, Doctor,' he said, shaking hands heartily.

To everyone's surprise the Doctor responded by flinging his arms round the portly swindler and giving him a generous hug. 'I too am eternally grateful to *you*, Garron,' he said solemnly.

Stuffing the red and white bundle into his overcoat pocket the Doctor shook hands with Unstoffe and then ushered Romana and K9 into the TARDIS. 'Cheerio,' he waved before slamming the chipped blue door shut behind him.

'Well, that's the end of that,' Unstoffe mumbled in a crestfallen voice, massaging his still painful shoulder. 'We'll just have to go straight from now on.'

Garron put his plump arm round the dejected figure beside him. 'Straight?' he cried. 'Come, come, my lad, we've not done too badly.'

Unstoffe stared at him. 'Oh, no,' he snorted. 'We've only lost the Jethryk and come out of all this carry-on without a penny. That's all.'

At that moment the amber light began to flash on the roof of the TARDIS. Garron and Unstoffe looked on in astonishment as the caked snow fell away from the shuddering structure in front of them.

Suddenly Garron's beady eyes widened. 'I never could stand the sight of that word,' he muttered with a shiver.

'What word?' Unstoffe frowned.

'P . . . O . . . L . . . I . . . C . . . E,' Garron growled, nodding at the faded lettering above the shimmering, wobbling box which was becoming more and more like a mirage every second.

They covered their ears as harsh elephantine groans issued from the violently vibrating woodwork, and then huddled together as the vortex sucked the surrounding air into a whirlwind storm of whipped up snow which tore fiercely at them like a multitude of invisible fingers. After a few seconds, only the flashing light remained visible. Then it too faded into nothing and everything suddenly grew eerily calm and quiet.

'So they *were* Alliance Security, after all,' Unstoffe muttered, breaking the ominous silence through chattering teeth.

'Who them?' Garron laughed, shaking his head pompously. 'Small-time privateers, my boy. Hopeless amateurs.'

Unstoffe threw him a puzzled glance. 'You must admit that was some getaway,' he protested. 'I've never seen anything like it.'

Garron shrugged. 'I'm glad they've gone. I was afraid the girl was going to twig.'

'Twig what?' Unstoffe demanded, exasperated.

With a smug grin Garron pulled something out of his furs. 'I swapped the Jethryk for a lump of flint, my boy, so we haven't lost it after all. Look ...'

'You cunning old ...' Unstoffe's jaw dropped as he stared into Garron's outstretched hand. Garron glanced quickly down and his fleshy smile froze. He was holding a hunk of ordinary stone.

'Well I'll be ... He ... He switched it back ...' Garron cried incredulously. 'I ask you, my lad. Who can you trust these days? Who can you trust?'

And the two tricksters stood staring at the useless lump of flint under the bleak midday sun like a pair of freshly made snowmen.

In the quietly humming control room of the TARDIS the Doctor unwrapped the nugget of Jethryk and gave it a thorough polish with the spotted handkerchief. Then he placed it carefully on the side of the instrument console, and, stepping back a pace with a gallant flourish, he invited Romana to carry out the transformation of the nugget into its true form.

Romana hesitated. 'Thank you, Doctor, but I should

141

not wish to appear presumptuous,' she smiled.

'I absolutely insist,' replied the Doctor, nodding at the Locatormutor Core in Romana's hand. 'You operate the gadgetry, my dear—I'll stick to the old conjuring tricks.'

Still Romana hung back. 'I am only your assistant, Doctor,' she murmured.

The Doctor arched his eyebrows in mock surprise and glanced hurriedly round the control room as if to ensure that they were not being overheard. 'Really?' he muttered. 'Well, I shouldn't boast about it if I were you.'

For a moment Romana looked as though she were going to smash the Core down onto the Doctor's head, but she managed to swallow her fury at his mischievous taunting.

Taking a deep breath, she slowly approached the console and held out the Locatormutor so that it just touched the Jethryk's glittering surface. She could not help glancing at the Doctor and he gave her a warm smile of encouragement. Cautiously, Romana switched the Core to mutation mode. They waited.

At first nothing happened. Then the filigree silver veins branching through the nugget began to pulse gently and to drain it of its intense indigo colour. Gradually the nugget became completely colourless, and then it began to glow so intensely that Romana and the Doctor were forced to avert their gaze as the glare increased to a searing, buzzing climax.

When at last they were able to look again, there on the console lay a large crystalline object clear as water with exact knife-edged facets and angles reflecting the light brilliantly.

Romana switched off the Core and sighed with relief.

'The first Segment of the Key to Time ...' the Doctor murmured approaching the console almost reverently. He took out his watchmaker's eyeglass and began to examine the Segment very thoroughly.

Romana suddenly gave a brilliant smile and put the Core away in her belt. 'Yes, the first Segment ... at last,' she said.

After a while the Doctor took out his eyeglass and put it back in his pocket. Then he rubbed his hands briskly together, and with cautious delicate movements wrapped the Segment in the spotted handkerchief.

'One down and five to go,' he chuckled. 'What about some tea?'

FANTASTIC
DOCTOR WHO
POSTER OFFER!

Pin up a magnificent full colour poster of Peter Davison as the Doctor, surrounded by a galaxy of Target novelisations – Free!

THIS OFFER EXCLUSIVE TO
DOCTOR WHO READERS